KILLER - OF - DEATH

ALSO BY THE AUTHOR ▼ *The Shaman's Last Raid*

Pictures by John Kaufmann

Harper & Row, Publishers   New York, Evanston, and London

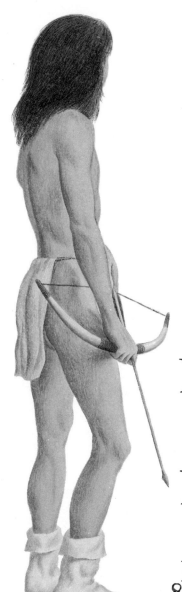

KILLER
- OF -
DEATH

By Betty Baker

CONTENTS

FOREWORD

The Continental Divide, that rocky ridge from which all rivers flow east on one side and west on the other, hugs the western border of New Mexico. Tight against the Divide on the east flows the Rio Grande and beyond that stretches the dreaded White Sands. On the west the Divide falls away into the hilly, canyoned desert of Arizona. This was Apache country, Mimbreño Apache.

In the mid-1800's it was also disputed country. The border between Mexico and the United States was somewhere in the southern portion of the territories of Arizona and New

Mexico. Just where no one was quite sure. Maybe some-place south of Tucson, maybe north of that town. The Mexicans pursued the raiding Apaches as far north as they could follow the trail. Wherever they turned back became the boundary for them. The Americans, busy with their mines in the northern mountains of Arizona, didn't worry about who owned the desert to the south. There was noth-ing there of importance.

Then plans began to take shape for a railroad that would stretch from coast to coast. The best route was through the southern portions of Arizona and New Mexico. The boun-dary must be settled once and for all.

The United States proposed the present border and offered to pay Mexico for any land she claimed north of it. This was the Gadsden Purchase. The Mexican government agreed to the purchase, but only after the United States promised to keep the Apaches north of the border and prevent raids on Sonora and Chihuahua. It seemed a simple task for the Army, but Easterners had no idea of the rugged vastness of the country or the nature of the Indians who lived in it.

In 1851 a survey party, followed by the Army, finally began to trace the border as we know it today. But other progress was slow. Two years passed before Congress at last approved the Gadsden Purchase, and in the meantime the Apaches had continued their raids. Angry and desperate, Mexico enforced her terrible Project of War, the payment of gold for Apache scalps.

Injustices followed misunderstandings until hatred con-sumed all hearts, "Mexicano," "white-eye" and those of "the

People." There was no peace until the Mimbreños and other Apaches were placed on the reservation in the White Mountains of Arizona in 1876. Even then Geronimo and his followers raced back and forth across the border, taking refuge from the Mexican Army by crossing into Arizona and escaping the Americans by crossing into the mountains of Mexico. But in 1886 Geronimo also surrendered.

Today some Mimbreños still live in the White Mountains of Arizona. The rest are on the Mescalero Apache Reservation in New Mexico, where they can gaze west across the glittering White Sands to the mountains their ancestors once roamed. If they have time, that is. For the Mescalero Reservation boasts ranches, lumber camps, a sawmill, a famous fire-fighting team, hunting, fishing, camping, skiing, a restaurant, a service station . . . and beauty. The prosperous reservation is a cool haven of spectacular pine-covered mountains tucked unexpectedly between two deserts. This now is the land of the People.

KILLER-OF-DEATH

 ONE

THE SCENT
OF
BIG GAME

I was born too late. Growing to manhood in the time of my grandfather's father would have made the heart sing. The country and all it contained belonged to the People. One's days passed in hunting, with an occasional raid against the Papago to relieve them of the burden of storing their harvest. Even better to have been born in my father's time, when easy raids against the Mexicanos supplied all the blankets, cookpots, horses and guns one needed. But if one is born to see what I have seen, it is better not to be born at all. For when the medicine woman strapped me to my cradleboard, sprinkled the sacred hoddentin and offered me to the Four Directions, the white-eyes were sneaking past the Cheyenne and creeping into our mountains.

I knew nothing of this until later. My early childhood was unclouded. I toddled after my elder brother and imitated his every act. Thus, sooner than most I received my first bow and arrow.

I was not yet sure of my aim when the season of Many Leaves came round. We moved into the dry country so the women could harvest the mescal. I followed my brother on his hunting trips, eager to bring in my share of rabbits for the cookfire. On the last of these hunts I led the way through an arroyo. My brother trod close on my heels, alert to my every mistake. My passage disturbed the sleeping rattlesnake, but when it struck, my brother took the poison.

He was the only child of my father's first wife. She tore her hair and gashed her legs until I wished that I had been the one following. To ease her sorrow my father joined a raid and captured a young Mexicano boy. The woman ceased her mourning. The boy was adopted by the People, and I found myself the elder brother, the one who must teach and lead.

The boy did well. Sooner than most he buried his memories and learned our tongue. None had a keener eye for a trail, and his skill with a bow soon exceeded mine. Only in two ways did he differ from the People. His eyes were blue, and when there was a race to be run or a message to be carried, he would mysteriously vanish. Many were the times I found him sleeping under the drooping branches

of a mesquite or curled in the shade of a cliff. Lazy Legs I called him, and the name clung like the two-horned thorns.

It was in my twelfth harvest that I first became aware that things were changing. Word came that three bands of white-eyes, larger than any that had come before, were camped in our mountains. The news disturbed my father and the other second chiefs. They talked long of what had happened to the buffalo-hunting tribes when the white-eyes moved among them. As for me, I worried only that exciting things might happen before I was ready to serve my warrior apprenticeship.

I trained harder than ever, running far into the desert and keeping my hand from dipping too often in my mother's cookpot. But the talk of war came to nothing.

The one the Mexicanos called Juan José gave word to leave the white-eyes in peace. Juan José was our great chief, so old that all those who knew his true name had joined the spirits. Everyone knows that with age comes wisdom, so his order was obeyed. But that order said nothing of the white-eyes' stock. When Ghost Face laid his chill over our canyons, more than one mule found its way into the cookpots.

Two harvests passed. The grumbling of the warriors grew louder. My father led more and more raids against the Mexicanos, but the white-eyes were like a forbidden pot of stew set before a starving man. I drove myself harder, determined to be ready when the time came.

Gian-nah-tah, the shaman's son, shared my ambition. He suggested that we try our skill against each other. Many were the traps and tricks we planned. All of mine failed. Nothing I thought of was clever enough to fool the shaman's son. Then, one night, a dream was sent to show me the way. I woke laughing. It was so easy. We were both eager to kill our first big game so we could begin our warrior's apprenticeship. Gian-nah-tah's own eagerness would lure him into my ambush.

I saved the deer hoofs from my father's next kill and waited for rain. Then I carefully laid a set of deer tracks into a small canyon where the rocks were known to hold a pool of water long after the smallest rain. There was only one way in or out of this canyon. Gian-nah-tah would not be able to resist rushing in for the kill. As I back-trailed, erasing my own prints, I saw that the track was good. Not too clear, and scuffed here and there where the "deer" had paused to scent the air. Anyone, except perhaps Lazy Legs, would be fooled.

Leaving no sign behind me, I circled and climbed above

the canyon. The sun rose high, then lowered. Still I hung over the rim of the canyon, my arrow ready in the bow. A boy's arrow with a button of buckskin on the tip. Released from a half-drawn bowstring, it would not wound. Only let Gian-nah-tah know that I had won at last.

As the sun lowered I began to think less of victory and more of the water jar before my mother's wickiup. But what good was all my training if I could not endure a little thirst? I would wait until morning if necessary. I knew Gian-nah-tah's habits well. Sooner or later he would cross the false trail.

After waiting so long, I was not happy when Lazy Legs threw himself down beside me.

"How did you find me?" I demanded.

He grinned. "It wasn't easy, but here and there you were careless."

"You could track an ant across a dry rock. Or do you follow the scent, like the coyote?"

"You don't mind running over half the country looking for a lost trail. I do. So I am sure I find the right trail and stay on it. It's easier that way." He peered into the canyon. "Where's the deer? Is it a big one?"

I searched his blue eyes, but it was true. My false trail had fooled him. Or perhaps it was only that he was intent on finding me and had not given it close attention. Just the same, it was something to have fooled him at all.

"Here is the deer. Here, beside you." I told him of my plan. "I hope your trail does not make him suspicious. Now be silent. This is important."

"I have news that is more important."

That made me sit up. "We are attacking the white-eyes!"

Lazy Legs shook his head. "No, it is bad news. Juan José has agreed to let the Mexicanos build a town in our mountains so that they can dig the pesh they call copper from the ground."

"I do not believe it." Not even Juan José was powerful enough to make us tolerate Mexicanos in the middle of our hunting lands.

"Our father is doubtful, too," said Lazy Legs. "He is going to Juan José to talk."

I glanced at the sun. There was still time to begin a journey today. If I were present, he might think to take me along. I began to rise. Lazy Legs gripped my arm and nodded at the canyon. Gian-nah-tah was hurrying through the thorny bushes, every muscle quivering with eagerness. He was too eager.

"Listen to that thrashing. If there were a deer, it would be beating itself in a frenzy against the canyon wall. Let us go."

As we stood up Gian-nah-tah let out a howl of rage.

I laughed. "He has discovered the food bag is empty."

Lazy Legs sniffed. "Not quite empty."

Then I also caught the smell. We stared at each other.

"But what is a skunk doing there at this time of day?"

"Perhaps it is thirsty," said my brother.

Gian-nah-tah heard our voices. He shouted and shook his fist.

"Ey, but your hunt has been good today," I called down.

"With game like that, you will be spending your two weeks alone in the desert much sooner than you thought."

I turned away, laughing. Lazy Legs trotted at my heels.

"This is very bad," he said.

"What is?"

"The skunk."

I laughed again at the thought of Gian-nah-tah's face. "It was an accident."

"But he will think you planned it. You have made an enemy, and the shaman's son is a bad one to have against you."

"Don't be foolish. By the time he returns to camp, he will be laughing about it himself."

"I do not think so. It is more than a trick with a skunk that he will hold against you."

Something in his voice made me stop and look at him. His clear eyes told me no more than the blue sky they reflected. "What else is there?"

"I am your brother."

"That I already know. Answer my question."

He turned quickly and led the way to the village. I puzzled over his words but could make nothing of them. It was but another of his mysterious fears of the shaman's son. Like bird tracks, they led nowhere. I pushed the matter from my mind.

They stood about my father's wickiups. All the important men of the village. The shaman was there, as he was everywhere something of importance happened. There were also Broken Nose, the fiercest of our warriors; Sons-in-jah, who knew the secrets of the sweat bath; Nah-tenah, father of five daughters, the youngest of whom had been casting strange thoughts upon me lately. There were others, but these I noticed as Lazy Legs and I halted at a respectful distance.

The shaman was speaking. "I have not forgotten how the Mexicanos have made slaves of the People. How they forced the men to scratch the pesh-klitso, the yellow iron, from the mountains. Our men toiled like badgers in dark holes. Many of them died. Our women were enslaved to grind their corn and tend their fields. They invited us to feasts of friendship and as we ate they slaughtered us like feeding ducks. Has Juan José forgotten?"

"He should remember better than most," said Broken Nose.

"That is true," murmured the others.

Juan José, when a boy, had been taken from our people by the Mexicanos and taught to read their strange papers. But Juan José sickened with grief for his family and the ways he had known, so he fled back to the People. When we captured Mexicanos with the strange papers, Juan José would read them. Always he knew what the Mexicanos planned and his raids were more successful than any other chief's. It had been many harvests since the People had dared to disobey his word.

"I will go and talk with him," said my father.

"I also will go," said the shaman.

"And you." My father nodded at Broken Nose. "We leave now. Perhaps we will not be too late."

The gathering scattered.

My father had always hung his weapons in the wickiup of Lazy Legs' mother. It was only right, as she was his first wife. I moved quickly to its door so my father could not miss me. Anxiously I waited for him to speak first.

"I cannot talk now, my son."

I made myself as tall as possible. "I wish to go with you."

"A chief cares for his people, not the other way around. You and your brother will stay. Together you can keep the cookpots filled until I return. My wives must not beg."

Ey, it was hard to reach manhood. Even harder when you were a chief's son. I stepped aside and said no more.

My little sister toddled around our wickiup, her short legs still jiggling with baby fat. She tugged at my loincloth and held up her toy cradleboard, the thongs dangling loose.

"What, again? Why must you always take the doll out? If you will not learn to tie, leave the thongs alone."

Her round face tilted up at me, her black eyes pleading.

"Everyone babies you too much. That's the trouble."

It was true. But such a pretty girl coming so long after two boys was bound to be fussed over more than usual. Both women spoiled her shamefully and my father, Lazy Legs and I were not much better. Even then I gave in to her silent pleading and took the tiny cradleboard. As I knelt to lace in the doll her face lit in a smile as lovely as the moon breaking through a cloudy night. No wonder she was spoiled.

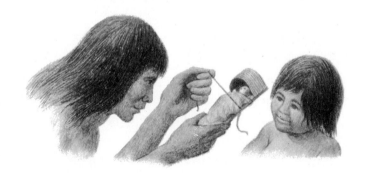

"Ah!" Lazy Legs' grinning face peered over my shoulder. "I was going to ask you to watch us shoot arrows, but I suppose you must grind your corn next and sweep out the wickiup."

I aimed a punch between his blue eyes, but he skipped easily away. Sharply his mouth closed on his laughter. I looked up and followed his stare.

Gian-nah-tah strode between the wickiups. I grinned until I saw the way he planted each moccasin heavily on the packed earth. His stocky body gleamed wet and raw from his efforts to scrub away the scent with sand and water. From the way people drew back, the odor was still strong. Or perhaps the smell came from the black-and-white pelt he swung in one hand.

I rose slowly and pushed my sister away. The shaman's son stopped an arm's length from me.

"I trailed my first big game today." His voice was dangerously flat. "It is the custom to give away the skin. I could think of no one more worthy than you to receive it."

He flung the skunk pelt at my feet, spun on his heel and stomped away, his quiver bouncing angrily against his back.

Lazy Legs said nothing. But as I looked at the smelling carcass, I remembered his words. *You have made an enemy, and the shaman's son is a bad one to have against you.*

TWO

DANCE OF
THE
RABBITS

The responsibility of providing food for two wickiups lay
heavy on my shoulders. As soon as my father and his companions rode off, I gathered what I needed for the evening's
hunt: the medicine bag with my charms and sacred hoddentin, a knife tucked into the top of my high moccasin, an
extra bowstring and a good supply of small-game arrows
with sharpened points. After a moment I added larger
arrows tipped with flint arrowheads. There was always the
chance I might find my first deer.

"Eat before you go," pleaded my mother.

I shook my head. "I want to be well hidden before the animals come to drink. Besides, I smell onions in the stew." The first thing one learned was never to eat onions before hunting.

"But you've had nothing since last night."

It did not matter. I had often practiced going without food for two days, sometimes three. But to please her I said I would take a bag of dried berries and parched corn. She bustled happily about the storage baskets, filling the deer-skin pouch so full that my loincloth sagged under its weight. When I walked, the bag thumped awkwardly against my leg. I called Lazy Legs from target practice. His stomach was always hollow as the shaman's drum. As I filled his cupped hands he eyed my quiver.

"Where are you hunting?" he asked.

"At a watering place I know."

"Is it far?"

"Yes, but we'll do nothing but sit when we get there."

He munched thoughtfully. I wasted precious moments waiting for his decision, but I was ever curious about the strange workings of my brother's mind. Any other boy would have fallen into step without a question.

I was glad I waited. Nah-tenah's youngest daughter, Shy Maiden, passed by with the water jug. She must have heard my heart thump, for as she passed, her eyes slid side-ways to me and she smiled.

"Nah-tenah will be a rich man someday," said Lazy Legs, "with five daughters and each worth many horses."

"It will be at least four harvests before I can think of a wife. And longer, most likely, before I have the horses to pay for one." But if I *were* old enough for a wife, and if I *did* have the horses . . .

Lazy Legs interrupted my dreams. "There's one who isn't worried about age or horses."

Gian-nah-tah stepped into Shy Maiden's path. She moved lightly around him. I could not tell if she smiled for him, but I didn't think so. He looked sourly at us before he followed her down the path to the stream. Even from where we stood we could smell the mint with which he'd rubbed his body. Mint for courting.

"The girl hasn't had her ceremony yet. The shaman's son shouldn't court her."

"The shaman's son does many things he shouldn't." Lazy Legs' hand groped in the berry bag.

I slapped his hand away. "Are you coming?"

"Is there enough left in there for two?"

I told him he could have my share. It was easy to fast these days. I had only to think of Shy Maiden with Giannah-tah and my hunger vanished like ground squirrels at the shadow of a hawk.

I led the way far up the small stream, climbing ever higher through the canyons. It was more than Lazy Legs had bargained for. I smiled, thinking of how he would tell of the trip tomorrow, making it sound as if I'd led him all the way to the Cheyenne country. But there was one good thing about Lazy Legs. He might complain and groan later or argue about going to begin with, but while on the trail he never shirked or complained. Truly, he was as much of the People as I.

We reached a place where the banks of the stream were wide and sloped gently to the water. Rushing floods had cleared banks of bushes, and small animals could drink without fear of ambush. We used the last of the daylight to circle and approach from downwind. We saw tracks of a raccoon and settled behind cover, confident of success. The ring-tailed one seldom strays from one hunting ground. I had trouble breathing light and slow, for this was the sort of place the white-rumped deer might come to drink.

Bows strung and arrows ready, we waited. As always happens when one dare not move, I began to itch in the most unlikely places. The moon rose. A full hunter's moon that made the bank gleam white.

Lazy Legs pressed his mouth close to my ear. "Have you noticed? No mockingbirds have sung."

It was true. The silence was not natural. Something upwind was frightening the game. But what? Not a coyote. A coyote was too clever to let his scent alert his dinner. But what other animal could command such fearful stillness? A lion!

My heart beat wildly. A deer was of little importance if I could bring in a lion's skin. I knew the big cat was even more cunning than coyote. But I reasoned that it might be too hungry to care. Or too proud to creep on its belly. I wanted the lion to be there. It must be there, waiting for my arrows.

I checked my bowstring, changed to a stone-tipped arrow and signed to Lazy Legs that I would scout the side of the canyon. He held me back until he untied the bag of food. Munching happily, he waved me on.

Keeping the slight breeze in my face, I crept silently away from the stream. It was easy until I reached a place where there was no cover except the shadows of young trees, thin stripes across the moonlit clearing. If I circled the clearing, my scent would surely be carried to the lion. For my mind had made a lion and a lion it must be.

It wasn't.

As I lay puzzling a way around the clearing, a fresh gust brought my nostrils the scent of mint. I crawled back to my brother.

"The shaman's son," I whispered.

"Ah, he wants us to go hungry so as to shame you before our father."

I agreed, but I thought that was but part of the truth. Everyone knew the shaman was ambitious for his son. Being my father's son did not mean I would be chief. True, I would be first in the council's thoughts, but if someone were better able to lead the band, I would be voted down. And if, standing on the edge of manhood, I could not provide the little meat necessary for two women, a tiny girl and my brother, surely I was not fit to step into my father's moccasins. Gian-nah-tah would fill them and take Shy Maiden to wife.

I clamped my teeth together. When my father returned, he would find the storage baskets full and all his horses alive. And no man would say he had fed us. If the great god Usen were willing, I added silently.

"We will get nothing here," I muttered. "Let us go."

"Go where?"

That was a thought.

"Look!" Lazy Legs pointed to the far bank. The coyote had caught our scent, for he looked our way, but he did not break his steady trot. "Brother coyote has important business."

I grinned. "And, like others I could mention, the only business he considers important is filling his stomach. Come." The coyote could well be Usen's answer to my prayer.

Without a backward glance, our four-footed scout led us up out of the canyon to a rocky mesa. Then down to a shallow valley strewn with rocks and tufted with grass. The full moon gave more light than the great ceremonial fire. Too much light for us to be mistaken about what we saw.

"Por Díos," whispered Lazy Legs.

The Mexicano words remembered from his baby days startled me. I envied him a little, for I had no words for what I felt.

Rabbits, more rabbits than all the boys in our village had ever killed in all their lifetimes, leaped crazily over the rocks, the grass and each other. Up, down, over and around. Here and there one would stop for a moment. Then another would soar over its back and off they would go, leaping and twisting.

"They look drunk," said Lazy Legs. "As if they are having the biggest tizwin party ever."

"I have heard the old ones talk of this. They say that sometimes, at the full of the moon, the rabbits gather to dance for Usen, the Giver of Life."

We watched in silence. Then my brother spoke the thought in both our minds.

"A dance to Usen is sacred. If we kill them, it will bring great evil to the People."

It was spoken as a question. I answered with a straight tongue. "I believe so, but I do not truly know."

The shaman tells us that evil spirits wander in the dark of night, taking the shapes of owls and animals. It could be that one had shaped itself to the form of our brother the coyote. Or it could be true what the Mexicano shamans told Juan José: That all evil spirits are in man himself. I do not know. Perhaps if my father had not left his family in my care; if Shy Maiden had not kindled a burning fire for greatness within me; if Gian-nah-tah had not pressed hard at my heels; if all these had not been so, perhaps my brother and I would have watched the sacred dance and returned to the village emptyhanded. But then, I think to myself, if the Mexicano shamans are right, it would have made no difference in what happened later. Truly, I do not know.

I know only that I said to my brother, "If Usen did not wish us to feast, he would not have sent the coyote to guide us. And, truly, he must be a spirit guide, for look how strangely he acts. He makes no effort to catch his meal, but sits quietly on his haunches watching."

I took hoddentin from my medicine bag and offered the

sacred pollen to the Four Directions. We each placed three arrows in the mouth, took two more in the hand that held the bow and fitted the shaft of a sixth to the string. The hum of our bows never ceased until our quivers were empty. Our wrists ached in spite of the leather wristbands. All but three arrows found targets. Thus we slaughtered the rabbits as they danced for Usen, the Giver of Life.

Each of us placed a rabbit before the coyote in thanks for his help. He did not look at them. He sat still as a stone, staring after us. I glanced back. It may have been only a shadow caused by the moonlight, but it seemed to me that he was laughing.

THREE

VICTORY
FOR
THE ENEMY

The village wondered at our burden of rabbits. Never before had two boys brought in so many at one time. As is the custom, we shared them with other families. Those whose men had gone on a raid against a ranch, widows and old ones with no one to hunt for them. I would have liked to carry some to Nah-tenah's wickiup so I could boast a bit before Shy Maiden, but it was Broken Nose who had gone with my father and it was his wives who received a share. To save unpleasantness, Lazy Legs took the two rabbits to the shaman's wickiup.

"I coughed until my throat ached," my brother told us, "but no one answered."

"Then they are visiting," said his mother, raking fresh coals over the roasting rabbits.

"I do not think so. There was whispering behind the blanket."

Our mothers looked at each other across the cookfire. There is one thing a boy learns early. When women talk to each other with their eyes, it is best to find them something else to think on. I looked around for something. My sister sat cross-legged, her elbows on her knees, staring at the fire.

"Look at the Little One," I said. "She sits with crossed legs, like a boy. When will she learn to be properly modest?"

"She is only a baby," said Lazy Legs' mother.

"She will learn soon enough," said mine.

I had meant it only as a change of thought, but when Lazy Legs said, "This morning she was whistling," I really began to worry. Baby or not, a girl must learn she's a girl.

"Show us how you can whistle," urged Lazy Legs.

Before I could stop her, the Little One puckered her lips and let out a tiny squeak of a whistle. I hid my laugh behind my hand, then scowled fiercely at her.

"Girls never whistle, Little One. It brings bad luck."

She put her finger in her mouth and lowered her head. In shame, I hoped, but I suspected she hid a smile.

"There is no child in this village as petted and babied as she is," I said.

Everyone agreed it was so, but when the rabbits were pulled from the coals, she was served with as much ceremony as a visiting chief. Lazy Legs skinned and cleaned his rabbit and gave her the tenderest portions. I did the same. After all, what could just one do against so many?

We settled in our sleeping robes with full stomachs. But would I find game tomorrow and would it be enough? So many rabbits and now there were only enough left for the meal tomorrow night. The dry branches and grass under the robe rustled as I tossed and turned. The fear of hunger gnawed inside as if I hadn't eaten. Not fear for myself, but for the women and the Little One.

True, the storage pits were filled with dried yucca and berries, corn we'd taken from the Mexicanos and rolls of thin mescal. But all this would be needed when the cold season came and Ghost Face kept the game in hiding. I could see that providing for a family was a great worry. I wondered how my father could laugh and joke as he did with this worry ever following at his heels like his shadow. And with the bigger worry of leading the band hanging over his head like a thundercloud.

I sighed and wondered if it wouldn't be better to join Lazy Legs under a mesquite and let Gian-nah-tah become chief. It would be what he deserved.

The coyote was just beginning his morning song to the pale sky when I stepped from the wickiup, my bow in my hand. Gian-nah-tah was waiting. He looked like a plucked bear standing there filling his broad chest with deep breaths and flexing his thick arms. Then he beat his chest and did running steps in place. A group of younger boys watched with open mouths. Lazy Legs was not among them.

Inside the wickiup, his mother called him. Silence, then a splash of water and Lazy Legs stumbled from the wickiup sputtering and dripping. The boys laughed and hooted. Lazy Legs grinned until he wiped his eyes and saw Gian-nah-tah. He glanced from the shaman's son to me. I put my bow and quiver away. If the shaman's son was waiting to trail me as he'd done the night before, there was no use going hunting. Later, perhaps, I could slip away.

"I will run with you today," I told my brother. I had outgrown the morning runs two seasons before, but it would do me no harm. "I want to see how well you train."

"And I also," said Gian-nah-tah. "These boys fresh from the cradleboards need someone to set their pace."

Lazy Legs flushed, but before he could speak Gian-nah-tah trotted off toward the flat thorny country. I moved up, trying to take the lead and guide the group of boys up the rocky slopes. Hill running made the chests large and the legs strong. It became a race between the two of us. Side by side we ran, leaping into a dry riverbed, stumbling, then clambering up the other side. From the shouts of the boys, I knew when they reached the arroyo. I glanced back. They were running well, but Lazy Legs was not with them. I let Gian-nah-tah run where he would and dropped back to look for my brother.

I could have wagered my best arrowhead that I knew where to find him. I would have won. A green-barked tree grew by the arroyo. Its branches drooped over the bank. When I raised them, there was Lazy Legs, calmly munching a strip of dried meat.

"Get up!" I shouted.

"But that wouldn't be fair. Look, the boys are returning."

"You have strange thoughts of fairness for one who pretends to run and doesn't."

"I agree. But I am always careful never to win. I wait until the last boy has passed before I return to the village."

He had no shame, that one.

"Don't you want to be a warrior?"

"Yes, but then I shall have a horse to ride."

"Not always." I dragged him out from under the tree. "Run!"

"As you say, brother." And he grinned, for he had no temper, either.

At that moment Gian-nah-tah led the boys past us and into the arroyo. Lazy Legs joined the group. Gian-nah-tah reached the top of the bank and stood there as the boys scrambled past him. As Lazy Legs climbed upward the shaman's son thrust his big moccasin into my brother's face and sent him tumbling backward to the bottom of the riverbed. I hurried down, but my brother was already on his feet.

"Why did he do that?" I asked. "It is the sort of thing one does to an enemy."

"To him, I am an enemy."

Surely Lazy Legs could not mean that Gian-nah-tah thought of him as a Mexicano. When a boy was adopted, he became one of the People. It did not matter that his eyes were blue and his head full of strange thoughts.

"To the shaman's son, everyone is an enemy," I said.

"Hah!" Lazy Legs trotted off.

I kept pace easily. "It is true. Everyone is his enemy. That is why he has no calling name."

A true name is a precious thing, not to be used every day like a cooking spoon but only on occasions of great importance. Some warriors used the names Mexicanos gave them for calling names. With others one had to be careful to say "that one" or "the old woman's grandson" or even "the one who rode out to hunt deer." Boys have no time for such speech. They call one another whatever fits best at the time, as we called my brother Lazy Legs. But no one ever called Gian-nah-tah anything but the shaman's son. It was shameful but true that we were afraid to call him what he deserved.

All that day and the next the shaman's son clung to my trail like a buzzard to a dying horse. My brother's skill with the bow brought us wood rats, rabbits and birds. Not enough to share. Truly, it was scarcely enough to quiet the rumblings in our own stomachs. But it saved us from begging or dipping into the stores or killing one of my father's horses. I promised myself never to push Lazy Legs into running again. What did it matter that he could not do everything? What he did, he did very well. But I prayed to Usen that he never be left on a raid without a horse.

While Gian-nah-tah rattled bushes and kicked stones to spoil my hunting, his own cookpot remained empty. I wondered how much water his mother would add to the stew before she put an end to his foolishness.

Then the warriors returned with a herd of horses and mules. All the village feasted, for no game is so sweet as mule well seasoned with victory.

The warriors sang of their raid, the weak heart of the enemy, their own cleverness and strong hearts. Ey, how I wished to be one of them! It seemed that I would never kill my first big game, that before I began my apprenticeship I would be as old as Shy Maiden's grandfather, who sat toothless and white-headed among the drummers.

Shy Maiden stood near, shouting praises to the dancing warriors. The meat turned to sand in my mouth when I remembered that she would soon have her rites of woman-hood. Before long one of these same warriors would tie his horses before her father's wickiup.

I wandered around the fire, but the shaman's son was nowhere to be seen. Nor did our paths cross the next day. Or the next. Then, as I approached the camp at dawn I heard laughter and shouting. I thought my father had re-turned. I had not seen the sentry's signal, but one cannot watch rabbit burrows and the sky, too. The rabbits still in my hand, I pushed my way to the center of the commotion.

Gian-nah-tah stood astride the carcass of a deer, his chest grown overlarge with pride as he boasted of the days and nights he had trailed the herd across the mountains. Ey, to hear him talk, one would think he was the god Child-of-Water slaying the monster antelope who killed with a look.

No one noticed me thrust my way through the cheering crowd. I threw the rabbits into my mother's wickiup and went to the place where the boys shot their arrows. No one was there. They were too busy listening to that lying coyote, Gian-nah-tah. I leaned against a tree scarred by target practice and thought how the shaman's son would soon serve his apprenticeship. Three raids and he would be a warrior. I slid to the ground and dug at the dirt with my knife. Lazy Legs came quietly and sat by my side.

After a while he said, "You cannot kill the earth."

I did not answer. It was not the earth I saw under my knife.

"You will dull your knife."

"Then I will sharpen it."

Silence. Then, "He gave the deerskin to Nah-tenah."

I stabbed so viciously that my fingers touched the ground. "It was Broken Nose who taught him to hunt. Not Nah-tenah."

"So people are saying. But Broken Nose is with our father, and Nah-tenah is the shaman's cousin. So people are also saying it is just that Nah-tenah receive the deerskin."

"That is not why he did it."

"No?" Lazy Legs picked up a grass-ring target and twirled it on his wrist.

"No. He knows that Shy Maiden will help to cure the skin. All the time she works, her thoughts will smile on the shaman's son."

"But perhaps Shy Maiden does not like to cure deerskins."

I snorted. "Of course she does. It is woman's work."

"Running down turkeys is boys' work and I don't like to do it. Your work has been to keep the cookpots full instead of trailing deer like the shaman's son, and you haven't liked it. Why should Shy Maiden like to cure deerskin just because she must?"

There was truth in that.

"So if she does think of the shaman's son," my wise brother went on, "her thoughts may be far from pleasant."

"That is so." I felt as if I'd just leaped into a cold stream after a long hot run. I jumped to my feet. "Throw the ring, brother. I'll show you how to shoot."

I held six arrows ready. Lazy Legs tossed the ring. I launched three arrows. Two soared through the grass circle before it reached the ground. My skill was not as great as some, but no worse than others. Eagerly I waited for my brother to ready his arrows. Never did I tire of watching him shoot.

He nodded. I swept my arm far back and tossed the ring high. Four arrows whished in ever lower curves, the last one but shoulder high. All four went cleanly through the target.

"Throw it again," he said. "Let me try five."

But as I swung my arm, smoke signals rose over the mountain.

"They are back!" shouted Lazy Legs.

I dropped the target and raced for the village. The three men rode in and everyone gathered to watch. They murmured at my father's solemn look, saying the news must be bad. But they waited courteously until he had eaten and smoked his pipe. Then, one by one, they came to sit by the fire. When the shaman and Broken Nose took their places beside my father, our chief spoke. He spoke long and of many things, as if at council, but it all skinned down to one thing. Juan José had signed a treaty. The Mexicanos were to settle in our mountains and dig the pesh called copper from the ground. The people sat in angry silence.

"It is but one town," said Broken Nose. "And what do they take? Some pesh from beneath the ground. It is nothing to us."

He wore a new red blanket and a silver bracelet. I wondered if they had made the town seem nothing to Broken Nose. I noticed my father and the shaman had no gifts.

"Perhaps it is nothing now," said Shy Maiden's father. "But we know what the Mexicanos are like. Give them the pesh from beneath the earth and soon they will want the earth, too, and all on it. Then they will demand the air above it. It is their nature."

"That is true," muttered the warriors.

My father spoke again. "Juan José has promised them safety on two trails leading to their towns to the south. They are to use only those trails and not leave their town."

"And if they do?" asked a young warrior.

My father smiled. "If they stray, we can only believe they are weary of life and wish to leave it painfully. They have been warned."

From the gleaming eyes around the fire I knew that the trails would be closely watched and that our warriors would visit often with Juan José's people. The Mexicanos had never kept a treaty. It was but a matter of time.

Time! How much time? Enough for me to be ready?

When the people had gone, I lingered at the fire, kicking at small stones and pretending I was busy with important matters. The women told my father the news. When they told him of my hunting, he said nothing. When they told of Gian-nah-tah preparing for his apprenticeship after killing a deer, he said nothing. It was not the custom to praise, but I had hoped he would tell me to prepare for a hunt. Instead he ordered me to bring my bow.

He held it to the fire and looked over it carefully. Then he nodded slowly.

"I will keep this for a time."

"But how will I hunt?"

"You have legs. Run down the rabbits and birds. When you are not hunting, have the old one help you make new arrows."

He meant Shy Maiden's grandfather. No man made arrows as straight and true as his. For three days I rubbed my legs with fat to strengthen them, but they still ached before the sun began its downward trail. It was good to sit by the old one and straighten the peeled wood on the hot stones. But the long hours of crouching over split feathers and wet sinew stiffened my legs. At sundown I hobbled across the village like an old man. Only Lazy Legs seemed to know how I ached.

"Rub your legs hard before you sleep," he told me. "It helps."

"It would help more if I could run in the afternoon. I have often run all day at a steady trot. It is the fast running after game, followed by long sitting, that makes them ache. It will pass."

Besides, it was soft and weak to ease pain. A warrior must be hard and strong.

Then one morning my father called me softly before first light. He led me into his wickiup. Lazy Legs snored lightly against the far wall. His mother smiled at me as she carried out the water jar. I held my breath. Could my sudden thought be true?

My father laid my bow in my hands. Rawhide had been glued along it to give more force to the arrows.

"Empty your quiver," said my father. "Take only arrows with stone arrowheads."

When I saw him lift the deerhead mask from behind his sleeping robe, I knew it was true. Armed with bow and gun, he lifted the blanket over the doorway.

"Come."

I stepped outside and offered hoddentin to the Four Directions. I also asked Child-of-Water, who had slain the four monsters, to guide my arrows. Then, my heart leaping high in my throat, I followed my father into the cool half-light of dawn.

FOUR

A BLACK
THREAD ON
THE BLANKET

I began to understand why Gian-nah-tah had been gone so long. We traveled back and forth one day and part of another before we found a track. I felt the inside of a print and crumbled the edges. Where the deer had trod on a clump of grass, I broke a stem and sucked it to test the moisture.

"Yesterday," I said. "About this time."

"We will follow. They graze slowly. We may find them tomorrow."

As we roasted quail that night I asked my father if game

had always been this scarce. It seemed to me that if it had, the People would have starved long ago or frozen stiff without warm skins.

"When I was a boy," said my father, "the game was as uncountable as the stars. When it became wise to the hunters, we moved to a new camp. There was always plenty."

"What happened to it?"

"The white-eyes came."

"There are but a few of them in the mountains. Surely they cannot eat that much."

"They hunt only with guns. The noise frightens the game and drives it away. Those that remain, especially the deer, are more nervous than ever."

"But we have guns." One of the first reasons for raiding was to get guns and ammunition.

"But the People use only arrows for hunting. It is something we learned when we hunted buffalo. We could creep into the herd and drop all we needed with silent arrows before the buffalo knew we were there. Also remember, the noise of a gun can be heard by an enemy as well as a friend."

My thoughts were still on the buffalo. The only one I had ever seen was a tattered robe in my father's wickiup. "Why don't we hunt the buffalo now?"

He looked past the fire, as if there were something in the shadows only he could see. "Those were the days when the herds roamed much of the country. It was a long journey for us. It led us into the country of the Cheyenne, but the herds were so large there was little danger of meeting the enemy. Then the white-eyes came. I have heard it said that the carcasses lay rotting and smelling as far as the eye could see."

"They did not dry the meat? Or take the strong tendons for bowstrings or the bladders for water bags?"

"They took only the tongues and the hides."

I tried to see the land strewn with wasted meat, but it was too strange a picture to draw in my mind.

"Now the buffalo are few and far away," said my father. "I hear that the Cheyenne are few also."

"The white-eyes?"

He nodded. "They bring sickness our shamans have never known. Death walks in their footsteps."

"Perhaps that is why Juan José ordered us to leave them alone."

"That may be." He killed the fire and we lay down at a safe distance from the dead embers. There was little chance that an enemy was near to see the fire, but a warrior learns to be careful. It was one more thing for me to remember.

The next day we came upon the herd. Seven deer, three of them fawns. My father offered me the deerskin mask. I would be sure of a kill if I put the deerhead over mine and, with the skin covering my body, crept among them imitating their movements. But Gian-nah-tah had not used a mask. Surely my skill was equal to his. I shook my head. The glow in my father's eyes showed he was pleased. We parted and began the hunt.

I pulled the red sweatband from my head and rubbed

my body with dirt. Flat on my belly, I squirmed forward one fingerbreadth at a time. A deer raised her head to look and test the air. I lay motionless until she had taken three mouthfuls of grass. Another turned and stared straight at me. I lay still and forced my mind onto thoughts of the sky and the short stiff grass. It was well known that thoughts can fly swiftly as arrows to warn game or enemies. I tried not to think so hard on the animals before me.

The shadows lay as long as the bushes when I was at last in range of a fine doe. But I could not risk a shot until she turned. Arrows ready, I waited. An ant scouted the sole of my foot and another tickled the back of my knee. I gritted my teeth and did not stir. Would she never move? Soon the deer would move to water and my chance would be lost. A fawn jumped and skittered at a butterfly. The startled doe turned. My arrow flew. She leaped. I launched another.

Hoofs glinted, white rumps flashed and the deer vanished. All but the one with my arrows, one my father had slain and the foolish young fawn. It nuzzled the deer I had shot and looked about uncertainly. It would starve without its mother. Better to slay it now. I fitted another arrow to my bow and let it fly.

My father called. He looked like a deer himself, with the antlered head and the deerskin covering his back. I signaled my success and set to work with great care. A mistake now could destroy my hunting skill for all time.

First I turned the heads of the deer to the east. Then, taking care not to step over the carcasses, I began the skinning, working quickly down the side to the rear of the doe.

When I had cut the meat into large pieces, I removed the intestines and put them to one side for Crow. Crow had once penned all the animals deep in the earth. Killer-of-Enemies, the brother of Child-of-Water, had released them so the People would not starve. But Crow could still work mischief on the hunt, and the intestines were always left for him. When the deer had been turned and skinned on the other side, I squatted beside it and ate the raw heart. I would have preferred the liver, but it was the custom to eat the heart of the first big kill.

My father finished with his deer and came to help with the fawn.

"We have done well," he said.

Too well, I thought. "How will we carry all the meat?"

"We will leave mine here and send someone back for it."

When the meat was bundled in the hides, he placed one bundle in the branches of a nearby tree.

"We have left you a feast, Crow," he called loudly. "As you eat, let nothing touch our meat."

I will speak true. When I told of my hunt before the village, the ants became scorpions. The herd grew large enough to cover the mountains and my skill so great I could have slain with a splinter. The laughter and cheers of the people swelled my heart and my story. Truly, it was a happy time. Shy Maiden's eyes sparkled. When I told of killing the fawn, too, Gian-nah-tah scowled and I boasted even more.

The women heated the large flat stones. When the slices of meat were cooked on them, the sizzling of fat was a song of victory to my ears. As we ate, I wondered who would receive the doeskin.

My uncle who had made my first bow and taught me its use had grown old and gone away. I owed no one else in the village except the old arrowmaker, but then Shy Maiden would have to cure it. I did not want her thinking angry thoughts of me.

"You must give it to the one who named you," said my father. "Catch two good horses, for we must seek him in the camp of Juan José."

As I obeyed, my wonder grew. Not for the cousin. Like all the People, I had many unknown cousins scattered to the Four Directions. But often I had puzzled over my strange name and how it had been chosen. I had never dared ask, for such things are not spoken of lightly. I could only hope he would tell me on the way. We camped. He said nothing of cousin or name. When we passed Juan José's sentries, I decided I would have to ask or go ignorant forever. But as our horses picked their way up the wooded canyon my father spoke.

"It was shortly before your mother's time came. My cousin rode into camp, something so unusual we knew at once he had news of great importance. He said he had been sent a dream of my son-to-be. It was a strange dream."

He was silent for a time. His face looked as it did when a warrior disagreed with him in council.

"And the dream?" I asked at last.

"The dream told that my son would never lead his people. But that the leader of our people would be slain and my son would return him to life."

So that was the reason for my strange name, Killer-of-Death. Strange in meaning, but stranger still because death was a word seldom used by the People. Only animals and enemies died. The People went away. I shivered.

"Truly, a strange dream," I said. "Could such a thing be so?"

"Only Usen knows. Stranger dreams than that have come to be known as true."

It gave me much to think on, but I had little time for thought just then. We entered the village of Juan José and my eyes were not large enough to see it all. Never had I seen so many wickiups. Our village would have to move five times to build so many. Iron kettles hung over the cook-fires, instead of the clay pots my mother used. Many women wore long skirts of gay cloth, and everyone's arms and ears were heavy with Mexicano silver. Ey, one needed only to use one's eyes to know why the Mexicanos had been allowed to build their town. I was sorry we had come, for already I had nothing but contempt for this unknown cousin who dreamed impossible dreams.

Women took our horses. Carrying the stiff deerskin, I followed my father to the chief's wickiups. Was this small wrinkled man the one I was to return to life? If so, it would be soon, for he was very old. I pondered the question as the men smoked and talked. Juan José offered us sleeping space outside his wickiup door, but my father refused.

"My son has come to see Red Sleeves."

I gasped. They stared at me, but I could not help myself. Everyone had heard of the warrior the Mexicanos called

Red Sleeves because of the white-eye shirt he wore. Everyone knew he was a giant of a man with a mind to match, and often I had heard what had happened when he took a Mexicano for his third wife. The brothers of his first two wives had protested. Red Sleeves had fought them hand-to-hand and slain them both with one knife. That had been the end of any grumbling against Red Sleeves. And this was the cousin who had named me.

I had always thought my father stood taller than our warriors because he was chief. For men take on the size of their deeds. But when I met our cousin, I knew that great size was in the blood, though none of our family ever reached the size of Red Sleeves. He towered above my father as the giant pine rises above the squat mesquite. I pitied the horse that must bear his weight.

Too awed to move or speak, I stared at this giant and the soft red shirt he wore above his loincloth. He nodded his massive head at the ground. My father sat. I stood dumbly clutching the deerskin.

"We have brought nothing," said my father. "Though there is deer meat on the horses."

Red Sleeves sent his wife to get it. My father looked up at me. I stepped forward.

"I also came emptyhanded, with only a poor deerskin your wife may find use for."

My father's nod of approval gave me courage.

"It was you who named me," I murmured as Red Sleeves took the deerskin.

My knees weakened and I sat down hard on the packed

earth. I do not know what we ate, for my thoughts were on the two men and their words. They laughed and joked about the Mexicanos and their ways.

My father asked, "When that red shirt is ragged and thrown away, what will they call you? Naked Back?"

My cousin laughed. "No, to them it will always be Red Sleeves—Mangas Colorado. You know the Mexicanos. When they get a thought in their heads, only gunpowder will remove it."

"Or remove them," added my father.

"In time, my cousin, in time. Never fear."

"When two lice move into one's blanket, it is an easy thing to catch them and crack them between the nails. But if one lets them breed, soon the blanket swarms with lice and one can never catch them all."

"That is true. But one can always burn the blanket."

"Then one goes naked and dies of the cold," said my

father bitterly. "Far better to kill the first lice and save the blanket."

Red Sleeves waved his arm toward the forest and canyons. "This is a large blanket. Big enough for all so long as the lice stay in their own corner."

"But they won't. That is not the nature of the louse." My father rose. "Mangas, hear my words and keep them close. This great land, this blanket, has sheltered the People from cold, hunger and enemies. The day may come when we must burn this blanket. I pray to Usen it will not happen. Think hard on it before you set fire to a blaze of vengeance. For, once this blanket is burned, there will be no life for the People among the ashes."

"I have heard," said the big man softly. "I will think on it."

As I followed my father to the sleeping place he'd chosen behind the wickiup, he asked, "You heard my words?"

"Yes."

"Remember them, my son. Dreams are not always true."

As I curled up against the chill mountain air, it came to me that presenting the deerskin was not the first reason for our visit to this camp. My father had wished both Red Sleeves and me to hear his words. It must mean that he thought we would lead the People one day. But what of the dream? Had my father no faith in dreams? That could not be. Dreams were messages sent by the gods. Everyone knew that.

A shadow flitted past. A horse whinnied and the shadow spoke soothingly. A sentry, on his way to keep watch over the Mexicanos. I shivered and turned my upper side into the warm place my body had made.

I wondered if the shaman's son had begun his fourteen days alone in the desert. I thought of my family and Shy Maiden. Then of Red Sleeves and what he'd said about the blanket being large enough for all. I wished I had a blanket. This forest was cooler than our sun-warmed canyons. I yawned and pondered my father's words also. Ey, so much to think on! It made the mind weary. Tomorrow was time enough for thinking. I hugged myself tighter, shivered once more and went to sleep.

The next morning we did not take the homeward trail, but rode into the rising sun. We came to a place where the mountain dropped away. The world spread out before us until stopped by a mountain range that looked like a dark thread woven between earth and sky. Before the mountains, the land gleamed whiter than a deer rump. That was the place of the white sand, where the gods painted pictures in the air that vanished when a man drew near. Closer to us another thread, a green one, marked the course of the great river. Along it, nearly at our feet, moved a black thread of carts, horses, Mexicanos.

"There are so many," I said.

"And this is only the beginning," said my father. "I have seen enough. Let us go."

A touch of the knee turned my horse after my father.

"Do we return to our cousin's wickiup?" I asked.

"We will go home and talk to the Little One. At least if she has foolish thoughts, she keeps them to herself."

We later learned that was the day the white-eye Johnson arrived in Juan José's camp and asked permission to trade with the People. Perhaps if we had returned, my father would have persuaded the old chief to say no. But then it would have made no difference, for the lice were already in the blanket.

FIVE

IN THE
DESERTED
VILLAGE

It was good to be around our own fire, with the women fussing over us, Lazy Legs talking through a mouthful of stew and the Little One, finger in mouth, waiting to see what we'd brought for her. I had forgotten a present, but somewhere along the trail my father had found a speckled feather. She stuck it into her black hair and did a side-stepping dance.

"Duck feathers would be prettier," said Lazy Legs.

Little One shook her head.

"Yes, they would," he insisted. "They'd shine green and

blue in the sun. And the long banded tailfeathers would hang down over your ears."

She turned to our father, her eyes bright, but he shook his head.

"Your brother is just hungry for duck."

"Not at all," said Lazy Legs. "I just think duck feathers would suit her much better."

His mother tried to shush him, but he was not to be quieted with a look or a pinch. Duck and duck feathers were all we heard until the Little One was hopping up and down in a frenzy of silent pleading.

"It is time she talked," said my father. "If she wants duck feathers, let her ask for them."

Lazy Legs knelt before her. "Say duck feathers. Duck feathers."

He said it slowly, over and over. At last the Little One looked up at our father, licked her lips and let out a piercing whistle. My father leaped to his feet, swept back the blanket of the wickiup and went inside.

"Is he angry?" asked Lazy Legs.

"A whistling daughter would make any man angry," I told him. "You can forget about roast duck."

But I was wrong. The next morning my father brought me the gourds.

"Do you remember the place?" he asked.

It was a pool beyond our old village, well off any trail we used now.

"Yes, but it has been many seasons since ducks swam there. We had to move because the game was frightened away."

"The white-eyes have taken all the beaver from there and moved on. The ducks may have returned."

"I will go."

The camp was awakening. Women called to each other as they prepared their day's work. Men who had not gone hunting were repairing bows or chipping arrowheads. The boys were beginning their morning run. Everything was as always except that Lazy Legs was already up and waiting for me. I shaded my eyes and searched the sky.

"What do you see?" My brother's blue eyes searched also.

"I am looking for snow clouds."

"Snow clouds?"

"If you are out of your sleeping robe this early, anything is possible."

He grinned. "I thought you were looking for the shaman's son."

"I hunt better without him." I waited, but he said nothing. I had to ask. "Where is the shaman's son?"

"He left for the dry country two days ago."

In twelve days he'd return, proving that he could find food and water in the desert as well as any warrior. Then, after serving on three raids, he'd be a warrior himself. And I was hunting duck feathers! I slung the gourds over my shoulder and stalked off.

"Wait!" called Lazy Legs. "Where are you going?"

"You wanted ducks, didn't you?"

"But our father was to go."

"He sent me."

My brother looked as if he'd lost his last arrow. "But you can't do anything."

For a moment I could only stare at him. Never before had Lazy Legs made little of me. "Don't worry about your stomach. I can catch ducks also. You'll eat well tonight."

He began to argue and plead, following me through the camp and causing everyone to stare. I turned on him in anger.

"Go back to sleep and leave me to do the hunting. Or take the gourds and get your own ducks."

He said nothing more and I turned away. The hurt look on his face made me angrier. What right had he to look injured when I was the one who'd been insulted? But my anger vanished as quickly as a rain pool under the hot sun. No one could be angry or unhappy on a day such as this.

Later it would be hot, but the coolness of night still lingered in the dim canyons. A breeze lifted the hair from my ears. Birds sang. A ground squirrel leaped to a rock and sat up, watching me curiously. Every sound and smell and stone told a story to eyes trained to see. Here a coyote had dug for his meal. There a wood rat had made a tiny trail to his nest. Life was all around and stirring.

I began to run just to feel the rocks and earth push back under my moccasins. My feet moved without effort, each one fitting against the ground as if the trail had been made for me. I flew forward, the breeze strong in my face. Joy and life surged up in my throat. I wanted to yell, let loose the scream that chilled the blood of our enemies. Instead I followed a ledge to the canyon rim and stopped, arms flung wide and head thrown back to the sky.

Silently, with my eyes, I thanked Usen for giving life to the earth. To this land that made the heart quicken. The land that bound the People so that when their time came they could not leave and their spirits walked between darkness and dawn, still part of the land that sang in their hearts and claimed them.

Then it came to me that our land did not belong to the People. The People belonged to the earth that fed and clothed and sheltered them. I dipped into my medicine bag and offered hoddentin to Usen, thanking him for giving me life among the People. For letting me live as a part of the land that made the heart glad. The land of the singing heart.

A spirit must have come on the breeze to warn me, for I realized that I stood against the sky, a clear target for an enemy. I dropped to my stomach and wriggled backward over the edge of the canyon wall. I trotted on, hoping no one had seen me.

There was the chief's son, they would say, standing big as a giant pine and asking for a bullet or an arrow. What kind of warrior will he make? Such a careless one is better left in camp. That was what they would say.

But, from the look of the trail, I had little to fear. No one came this way. The old village was deserted and forgotten. I searched for landmarks. The place of the ducks was near. I left the faded trail and picked my way around the village. I had spent my childhood there. I did not want to see it now, left to the rats and the snakes.

My father was right. The ducks had returned. Not many. Two males with bright feathers, their five drab wives and ten or so little ones. I decided to take one male and two females. I did not care for the taste of duck, nor did my father. Three would be enough, the male providing the gay feathers Lazy Legs had made our sister want.

I made my way upstream from the flock and set the gourds in the water. Then I crossed over, picked my way downstream and waited for the gourds to float in to shore. Their passage sent the ducks fluttering and squawking, the mothers swimming madly in circles and calling for the little ones. Again and again I carried the gourds upstream, set them afloat and waited for them to drift ashore. At last the ducks were accustomed to them. If a gourd bumped into their rumps, they jabbed angrily at it and went on with their feeding.

I collected the gourds for the last trip. I hid my bow and

quiver on the bank and put the large hollow gourd over
my head, turning it so that my eyes could see through the
holes cut in its side. I slipped into the water. It was low,
hardly to my armpits. I set the other gourds afloat. Crouching low in the water, I bobbed and drifted as the gourds
around me drifted and bobbed. The male twisted his head
to preen his back feathers. I bobbed near, grasped his legs
firmly and jerked him under water in a quick motion. In
a moment he hung limp in my hands, the current tugging
him gently underwater. I drowned the two females as
silently, made my way to shore and collected the gourds.
The other ducks gave no sign that they noticed their companions were missing.

I wondered if other game had returned here now that

the white-eyes had taken away their booming guns. I set off up the stream, looking for a place where game came to drink at the water's edge. All animals needed water and they returned night after night to their favorite banks. Their tracks, if I found any, would tell me if hunting in this area would be worth the trip. It was always well to know where one could put an arrow in a meal.

I found nothing and was ready to turn back when, at the edge of the water, I saw a ridge left by a heel sunk deep in the mud. A moccasin heel. I would have thought nothing of it if the bank had carried other tracks, but there were none. Eyes close to the ground, I crept back and forth. Someone had taken great care to brush over his trail. Who? Surely not an enemy. Nothing could enter our country that a scout or sentry did not see. Why would one of the People cover his tracks?

I hid the gourds and ducks between two boulders and set off to find the answer. Back and forth I went, head bent to my knees, eyes searching. There! A stone with dried dirt clinging to the top, turned clean side down by a careless foot. Another. Then a single short white thread caught on a thorn. It was clear that the person who wished to be hidden had gone to the old village.

I dropped to the ground. Making use of every rock, bush and dip, I wriggled forward to where I could see the old wickiups. I had approached from the east so I could see the entrance of every wickiup. Or, rather, the entrances of those still standing. Many were only heaps of sticks. The grass covering on others flapped and swayed in the light breeze. Broken pots, warped arrow shafts and bits of ragged cloth strewed the once neat space in the center of the village. The musty smell of rotting wood hung over everything.

I lay still, my eyes trying to see everyplace at once. A lizard darted from one ruin to another. A snake worked its way around an old storage basket, following the shade. Bees hummed steadily. The village was as deserted as it looked, for the little creatures were undisturbed. Then why would any of the People come here? To seek shelter while on the hunt or to see if the game had returned. Many reasons for a warrior to pass through. I frowned. Nothing explained why anyone would hide his tracks unless he were a thief. What was here to steal?

Alert and watchful, I crept from one wickiup to another. In the third one I found the answer. Tucked behind the lashed cross-pieces were pouches of food. Corn, dried berries, dried meat. And on the pouches was the quillwork design used only by the shaman's wife. Inside were many tracks, each with the deep heelprint made only by Gian-nah-tah.

I squatted on my heels, ready to leap up if someone came, and thought on the meaning of what I had found. Food in an abandoned wickiup and a carefully covered trail to water. Ey, the shaman's son had prepared well for his fourteen days in the desert. He was a cheat who shamed his People. If the council knew of this, he would never become a warrior. I must tell my father. I rose, then sank back on my heels.

What could I tell my father? That it seemed that Gian-nah-tah was not living in the desert by his skill and knowledge? The pouches could have been left here any time. Gian-nah-tah could say they were from the time he'd hunted the deer. The heelmark by the stream would be gone by the time I brought my father to see, and the trail now carried my own markings. Gian-nah-tah was the sort who would stand before the council and say I had done it all out of spitefulness. After the accident with the skunk, who would disbelieve him?

There was one thing I could do. I grinned as I pulled down all the food bags. I would make Gian-nah-tah earn his apprenticeship whether he wanted to or not. I searched carefully, but there was no other food supply in the village. Carrying all I had found, I left the dead sight and smell of the lonely sagging village behind me and trotted back to collect the gourds and ducks.

Ducks! I stared at them, remembering Lazy Legs' words this morning. *Our father was to go. You can't do anything.* My brother knew. For once, when he said he was not interested in food, he was speaking the truth. He knew our father could not take the word of a boy. Especially against the shaman's son. So Lazy Legs had put the request for a duck hunt where my father would not refuse—in the Little One's eyes. My father would have seen and known the truth as I did. But he had sent me alone. My word was no better than Lazy Legs'. I had done the only thing I could do.

Heavily burdened, I took the homeward trail, grinning as I thought of Gian-nah-tah's face when he found his precious stores gone. Well, it could happen to the best of warriors. We would soon see if Gian-nah-tah was truly the great hunter he claimed to be.

Lazy Legs waited outside camp in a little cave under a red rock ledge. He darted out to meet me.

"You sent me after duck to catch a coyote," I said. "How did you know?"

"The day the shaman's son left for the dry country, I came across his trail. He is the only one who puts his heel down hard in that certain way. I wondered what he was doing in the mountains, and I followed. You know what I found."

I handed him Gian-nah-tah's stores. "Here, you can feast for days. But destroy the pouches when they are empty. I have made an honest warrior of the shaman's son."

"You have also made him angry."

"He will never know who found his secret."

"Perhaps not, but he will guess."

His words worried me. But the worry soon passed, for my own time in the dry country was near. I looked forward to it eagerly, for afterward I would serve my apprenticeship on three raids against the enemy. I was too busy preparing to think for long on the shaman's son.

There was a new bow to be formed and seasoned in hot ashes, new arrowheads to be chipped bit by bit, more things to be learned from my father. And all with Little One watching wide-eyed at my elbow, her seeking fingers forever in the way. I did not mind. I was too happy to care about such little annoyances. Then Gian-nah-tah returned.

He limped into camp at sundown on the last of his fourteen days. His thick frame was thin and drawn, like an old skin hung on drying poles. His moccasins had been mended so often that the tops came only to his ankles. His loin-cloth had been ripped to bandage a bloody gash on his leg. Like it or not, he had proved himself. He could live alone in the desert if he were cut off from his raiding party.

The village celebrated. I cheered with the rest, for only Lazy Legs and I knew how truly hard it had been for Gian-nah-tah. But when he passed by, the look he gave me was one of pure hatred.

He knew my own time was near. Would he take revenge when I was alone? Stalk me and wait until I was weak with hunger and thirst, then shoot me? No, he would not leave an arrow wound to cast suspicion. He would wait until I lay asleep or exhausted and then mash my head with a rock. *The Papago found him,* everyone would say. And our people would raid the Bean People and take revenge which would not ease my spirit one bit.

Lazy Legs' thoughts must have followed my own, for he asked, "Does everyone return from his days in the desert?"

"Everyone who is worthy," said my father.

I gazed at the shaman's son and wondered.

SIX

MY TIME
COMES

Sons-in-jah chanted the sacred songs as he built the sweat-bath wickiup. When the pit was ready and the four hot rocks had been carried in on forked sticks, Sons-in-jah rubbed my naked body with fragrant leaves and made me drink the sacred broth. He held back the blanket until I found my place against the far wall, facing the door and the rising sun.

The blanket fell, closing off all light. Water hissed on the hot stones, sending rolling steam upward in great wet clouds. More water. More steam. I was drowning.

I clawed my throat, gasping for breath. Then I forced myself to overcome my panic and breathe short gaspy breaths through my mouth. I was not sure whether I was breathing or drinking, but I was doing well until Sons-in-jah commanded me to sing.

Sweat rolled down my back and from my armpits. It tickled and itched, but I'd dropped the scratching stick and could not find it in the clouds of steam. I clenched my hands on my knees, for to scratch with the fingers in the sweat bath was forbidden. Weakly I gasped the chant between quick breaths that wrung just enough air from the steam to form the words. When I thought I could bear it no longer, Sons-in-jah pulled aside the blanket. I stumbled out.

The warm air hit me like an icy blast. I took great deep gulps as I raced down to the small pool in the stream. It was too shallow for swimming, but I rolled gratefully in the water. Pure water below and pure air above, with no unnatural mixing of the two.

I slept well and woke next morning eager to be on my way. The family gathered to see me leave. As always, Lazy Legs crept out last. He carried a sifting basket in his hands.

"Look," he said. "I put fourteen pine nuts in this basket. I will eat one each day. When the basket is empty, it will be time for you to return."

My father snorted. "Cactus will grow rabbit fur before you learn to keep your hand from a food basket. In three days you will have eaten them all and be wailing that your brother is lost."

Everyone laughed. Even I, though the thought of not returning added a strange note to my laughter.

I checked myself again to be sure I'd forgotten nothing. Quiver, bow case and bow. Knife in my moccasin top, a bone awl for mending the moccasins, a fire drill and my medicine bag. No food and no water. All was ready.

My father blew hoddentin to the Four Directions. My mother pressed a piece of turquoise into my hand. The blue stone was the strongest of medicines. Silently I turned away. Atop the last rise I looked back. They were still watching. Smiling, I trotted into the canyon. The sentry rose to stand against the sky and lift his rifle in farewell. He was the last person I was to see for fourteen days.

The first day I found water but no food. The women roam far and wide after nuts, berries and seeds. As soon as the harvest ripens, the women have stripped the country bare. Boys eat their fruit green or go without, at least when within a fair distance of the camp. The second evening I ran down a rabbit and fell asleep wondering why Giannah-tah had been afraid to spend his time here. Four days later I knew.

The heat of the sun on the rocky ledges around the camp was as nothing to the heat in the open desert. It was the season of Large Leaves, when lizards and snakes sought shade early in the day. Clouds formed and dropped rain over the mountains I had left, but no rain fell in the dry country. Not yet. Lizards and grubs were easily caught, but did nothing for my thirst. I trudged to every thin green line that meant a stream only to find each one dry. At last I chopped open a short round cactus. Eagerly I stuffed my mouth with the white pulp, sucking it dry of moisture. It was sickening. I gagged and retched. My stomach emptied.

Again and again I tried until some of the juice rested uneasily in my stomach.

After a short rest I went on. My back seemed to be crawling with insects. As the sun dipped, the feeling grew stronger and the hair on my neck rose. I forced my legs to hold the slow trot that covered ground fast without tiring. Over and over I told myself not to look back. A flat-topped ridge broke the rolling desert. Anxiously I eyed the sun. Would I have time to pass the ridge and climb it from the other side before the light failed? I dared not run faster. In no way could I let the person I felt was following know that the spirits had warned me.

Slowly I changed my path to lead behind the ridge where the rocky base would hide me from my follower. When I thought I was out of sight, I spent my last breath on a dash for the rocky hill. Loose rocks and jagged boulders covered the hillside. Climbing was hard, but I dared not rest. I was racing the setting sun. As I pulled myself to the last ridge, there was a sound like the rattle of dried beans in a pod.

It was coiled in the shade, partway around the rock I clung to. The fork tongue tested the air for the bold creature that had dared disturb its rest. The warning rattle sounded again.

A rattlesnake . . . someone following . . . the memory of a dry arroyo and my brother at my heels. Dimly my mind told me it was not the same, but rage at the creature before me grew and shadowed all reason. My hands clawed loose a rock and threw it at the arrowhead of the snake. Another

and another, until the snake lay silent under a heap of stones. My mind cleared and my legs grew weak with fear. I had killed one of the sacred creatures.

Trembling, I drew the smooth blue stone from my medicine bag and sat holding it tightly as I prayed for protection against the unknown evil that would befall me for my crime. Below in the desert I had just crossed, a shadow moved from bush to bush, disappeared into a hollow, then reappeared nearer the ridge. A shadow with broad shoulders and short heavy legs. The shaman's son seeking revenge.

Vengeance! I clutched the blue medicine stone. In killing the rattlesnake, had I not taken vengeance for my brother struck so long ago? Among the People no law was greater than the law of vengeance. A life for a life. It was stronger than the law that forbids the killing of sacred creatures. Had not Broken Nose killed a grizzly bear when it attacked him? After the shaman had sung over him, the village had praised his strong heart. And that had not been for revenge. I rubbed the blue stone. No evil would come to me, I was sure. Unless it came from Gian-nah-tah. I glanced around. Where had he gone?

Eyes straining in the dim light, I searched the country below. There was nothing that did not belong. Cautiously I crept along the top of the ridge. There he was, picking his way carefully among the boulders. I counted on my fingers. More than half my time to go yet. I would never survive with the shaman's son threatening me. I watched to see where he would reach the top, then crawled back to the dead snake.

One by one, I removed the rocks I had thrown. The head was crushed and the body flattened in places. But how to carry it? Everyone knew that the touch of a rattlesnake skin would cause a man's skin to peel off, leaving his flesh bare and red like a skinned deer. There could be no death more horrible. I remembered Sons-in-jah carrying the hot stones into the sweat bath. With two arrows I lifted the dead snake and carried it to a place I thought would be just above Gian-nah-tah's head. I waited.

No sound betrayed him. It was a shame he was to die. He would have made a fine warrior. I could hardly see where one rock ended and another began. A few more heartbeats and it would be dark. Gian-nah-tah moved below me, a silent shadow. I raised myself to my knees, lifted the snake with the arrows and dropped it on the shaman's son. He grabbed, held it a moment in his hand, then saw what it was. His scream stopped my heart. Never had I heard such terror. He screamed again and again as he tumbled down the hill.

I clasped my ears to shut out the sound. But all night his cries echoed in my head as I lay sobbing on the rocky hill.

The rest of my time in the desert runs together in a memory of sun and heat, mouth swollen with thirst and mind haunted by the ghost of Gian-nah-tah as I wove my way back and forth, trying always to reach the mountains and seeming never to get closer. I reached the first canyon on the fourteenth day. I would be a day late, perhaps two, reaching the camp.

That night thunder shook the ground. Great spears of lightning struck the mountains above me. The storm did not reach the lower hills, but the stream near me flowed deep for a short time. Long enough for me to drink and wash. I dug up a yucca root and washed my hair, using the spiny edges of a leaf to comb it roughly. My moccasins hung in tatters, but my loincloth was now clean and in one piece.

The parts hanging front and back were longer than before, so I knew I must be thinner, but at least I would look better than . . . someone else who had returned. Even in my mind I could not say his name.

Then it came to me that my mother might be mourning her lost son. I was wasting time instead of hurrying to save her grief. I left my bow unstrung that day and did not hunt. When the sun went to his sleeping blanket in the west, I stopped to drink and rest, then moved on. Bats swooped and soared around me. Startled rustlings told of small night creatures disturbed by my passing. The moon rose, a thin weak moon that gave little light but marked the direction I must take more clearly than the stars.

Above me a coyote howled, the cry ending with an extra note. I answered and the hidden sentry let me pass into the canyon that led home. The cookfires were dying coals. A dog roused to growl, caught my scent and went back to sleep. It was the only greeting I received.

Silently as an enemy, I crept into the wickiup and stretched out on the sleeping robe. Ey, how good it felt after the hard ground! I breathed deeply of the good smells and smiled, thinking how surprised my family would be in the morning. Then, light as the smallest of insects, fingers moved over my face and body, pausing to feel tenderly the scratches on my legs. With a small sigh my mother returned to her sleeping place on the other side of the wickiup. She could not have been sleeping or she would not have heard me enter. I was glad I hadn't waited until morning to return. The worried touch of my mother's hands was a greater welcome than the cries of the village.

I slept and the ghost of Gian-nah-tah walked in my dreams. His spirit had been with me ever since that night of the snake. When I stepped out in the morning, I was not surprised to find it waiting in the camp. But when it stepped forward, eyes glittering, and greeted me with words, I turned and ran until my legs could run no more. I threw myself face down, shaking and gasping for breath. I do not know how long I lay there before a hand touched my shoulder. I yelled and rolled away, trying to get my feet under me to run.

Lazy Legs laughed. "What is the matter with you?"

"It isn't a laughing matter." I looked around. "Where is it?"

"Where is what?"

"The spirit of the shaman's son," I whispered.

"I think you had better let the shaman sing over you. You are very sick."

"No, not the shaman! He would not cure me. He must know I . . ."

"You what? What is it, brother?"

I licked my lips, leaned close and whispered, "I killed the shaman's son."

"You are sick. The shaman's son hasn't gone away. He struts around the village as arrogant as ever." He was silent a moment. "He was gone for a time after you left. Did he follow you?"

I told him what had happened. "His father must have made strong medicine, for the curse has not worked. If that was truly the shaman's son I met, his skin is in one piece."

"The Mexicanos sometimes wear bands of snakeskin on their hats," said my brother.

"And what does that mean?"

"Nothing, except that they manage to keep their skins."

"The Mexicanos are evil to begin with." I walked away, for I did not like the thought that had just come to me. The laws of the People had been made by the gods. They were not to be questioned or doubted. But when I stopped to watch Gian-nah-tah wrestling, the thought flitted again through my mind. I shook it away.

"His father is a great shaman," I said softly. Silently I added, *I must be careful not to anger him.* I determined to bury deep all memory of my time in the desert.

Though I now stood at the edge of manhood, the seasons passed with little change in my life. There were a few things. During Shy Maiden's rites I noticed one of the black-masked g'ans danced on legs that were crooked and bowed like Sons-in-jah's. And the one masked spirit who danced alone and mimicked the others, wasn't he Chato, who was well known for his wit? For the first time it came to me that the masks and tall wooden crowns were worn by men and not spirits. With that the g'an dance lost its mystery. But perhaps that is part of the hardship of being a warrior.

Not that I was a warrior yet. The gods had been good to the People. The storage pits were many and full. Hunting remained good within a day's journey, and there was little need for raiding. During the season of Earth Is Reddish Brown one raid was made on a Mexicano town to get cloth, guns and corn. Gian-nah-tah went on that one, but I did not volunteer. My father led the raid, and I did not think it right that I should serve my apprenticeship on his raids. Better to let someone else boast if I did anything worthy of boasting. The shaman's son also joined a raid while he was visiting in another camp. So it was that when Ghost Face slowly gave way to the season of Little Eagles, Gian-nah-tah was ready to serve his last raid of apprenticeship and I my first.

I was glad this was so. For Gian-nah-tah was already familiar with the language and duties of apprenticeship and the shaman could instruct me alone. Not that Gian-nah-tah and I had been fighting, but ever since our days in the dry country there had been a tenseness between us. We met only when we could not avoid it, and then we circled and eyed each other warily like strange dogs.

All during the cold season I had sat for a time each day with the shaman learning special words, special duties, things I must do and too many things I must not do. My head buzzed and still I crammed more and more into my weary mind.

Then one day I saw Chato, the young warrior who danced with the g'ans, lead four horses to Shy Maiden's wickiup and tie them there. Day after day I watched the wickiup, all thoughts of the shaman and raiding gone from my head. I could think of nothing but Shy Maiden and her sweet way of looking up at me through her lashes. But the horses remained tied. Shy Maiden did not feed and water them, and Chato's uncle led them away.

After that I listened more carefully to the shaman, determined to become a great warrior with many horses and blankets. But it would have to be soon. Shy Maiden would not be living long in her parents' wickiup. Now I was sorry I had not begun my apprenticeship on my father's raid. Gian-nah-tah would have horses before I did. There are times when too much pride can be a heavy burden.

Then, early in the season of Little Eagles, Broken Nose rode into camp with exciting news. The Mexicanos were straying from the two trails Juan José had laid out for them.

"Once every moon," said Broken Nose, " a string of many wagons comes from the west. It travels many days before it reaches the safe trail. We will be gone a long time, but the guards are few and the wagons many and well filled. The risk is small. Who will join me?"

My feet shuffled impatiently as the men asked questions and talked among themselves. Lazy Legs darted in and out among them. He saw me and came to ask if I would join this raid.

"I will if these weak-hearted warriors ever stop their everlasting debate."

"It is a grave decision. A man should only risk his life for something worth while."

I tried to snort like my father. "A man can find a rattlesnake in his sleeping blanket and be struck down."

He looked at me anxiously. "I have never heard of such a thing. Have you?"

"No. I only mention it to show that if a man can be sent away by so many things in his own wickiup, why should he hesitate about risking his life on a raid?"

Lazy Legs sighed. "I am glad to hear that."

I was sorry I hadn't thought faster and told him that such accidents happened often. Every day, in fact. It might have brought him from his sleeping blanket at a respectable time.

At last four warriors stepped forward. Then two more. My father was not among them. Eagerly I stepped up, half afraid Broken Nose would refuse to take me.

But he nodded and said, "That is good. With both of you, we will surely have good luck."

I turned my head. Gian-nah-tah stood at my shoulder, volunteering to finish his apprenticeship. As I stared, he looked at me and smiled. His eyes were cold and the smile on his lips held no laughter. It reminded me of something. But what? Halfway to the wickiup I remembered. Gian-nah-tah's grin was the same one the coyote had worn the night Lazy Legs and I had killed the rabbits. It was not a pleasant memory. I pushed it away and prepared myself as best I could when I had no knowledge of the trail ahead.

SEVEN

THE FIRST
RAID

The fire crackled and filled the air with the sharp scent of burning mesquite. Everyone in the village stood waiting. The shaman was taking longer than usual. Perhaps the spirits were too busy to answer. Or, worse, perhaps the signs were bad and he would forbid the raid. At last his medicine hat bobbed above the heads of the crowd. The people parted and the shaman stepped into the firelight. He wore the buckskin medicine shirt painted with the sacred symbols. In his hand was the medicine cord of four strands. He walked to the center of the open space around the fire, raised his arm and spun the medicine cord in a great circle over his head. As he chanted, the cord slowed. The four strands dropped over his shoulders as the last word of the chant faded into the darkness beyond the fire.

"I have consulted the spirits," he said. "I have climbed the mountain and listened to their voices. I have drawn the circle and read the signs."

He paused, turning slowly to look into the faces of the raiders. My toes squinched inside my moccasins. Would he never speak?

"The raid," he shouted, "will be a victory for the People."

I threw back my head. The scream that had been building poured forth, lost in the shouting of others. The drums spoke. Broken Nose leaped into the circle and began his dance, showing how the raiders would scout the wagons, creep forward on their bellies and then strike. One after another, the raiders joined him, each showing how he would slay the Mexicanos and drive off the mules laden with guns, knives and food. They twisted and turned their red-and-black-painted bodies. They shot arrows at the stars and

stabbed the air with their knives. Then they trotted about the fire, beating their feet hard in the rhythm of horse hoofs and showing how great would be the loot they brought. The women shouted and cheered, just as they would when the raiders returned.

The dance ended. The women herded their children into the sleeping blankets. The warriors soon followed, though there was time for little sleep before dawn. I knew many of them would not try to sleep, but would sit in the dark watching and listening for signs, good or bad. I thought I would not sleep either.

I lay there seeing myself doing all the things the raiders had acted out in their dance, though such deeds could not be mine until I'd served on three raids. I sighed, thinking of the shaman's son. His time would be ended. Mine was just begun. How would it be with the two of us so close for so many days? We were not to speak unless necessary. That would help, but I wished Lazy Legs were old enough to go in Gian-nah-tah's place. Perhaps then I would not have this crawling feeling in my stomach. But, then, it was my first raid. Strange feelings were to be expected.

When I woke, the mountains loomed dark and lumpy against the paling sky. I slipped the thong over my head so that the drinking reed and scratching stick dangled over my chest. A water bladder and a pouch of food were all I was allowed to take. I felt naked without my bow and quiver. My right foot lifted too freely without the weight of my knife.

My mother lay watching. I pretended not to notice, but

as I stooped under the blanket, I could not help looking back and smiling. For a moment I wished the Little One would bounce up and ask for something in that silent way of hers. Anything to hold me here another moment or two. It was not the way of a warrior but, then, I was not yet a warrior. Only an apprentice. I lost the shame of my soft feelings when I found my father wandering around the wickiups brandishing a stick and muttering about dogs that ruined a man's sleep. I smiled, for no dog had so much as whimpered that morning. I would have liked to know if he watched us out of sight, but it was forbidden to look back. Somehow, I believe he did.

I was glad our party was small and on foot, for Gian-nah-tah and I traveled in the rear and the dust from horses would have made our throats raw. Also, the dust would have warned the enemy as we trailed the wagon train across the desert. That was, I decided, the reason for traveling on foot and I felt proud at having thought it out by myself. But pride does not last long when you have much to learn and someone like Gian-nah-tah is there to remind you of your ignorance.

Not that I didn't know what was expected of me. I pulled grass for the warriors' sleeping places, served the food and carefully called it coyote meat, just as the wagon train was called the herd of deer. The language of the raid was diffi-cult. I talked as little as possible even when Gian-nah-tah complained that the grass I gathered was full of thorns and that our food would soon be gone if I didn't measure more carefully. When the warriors finished, we ate by ourselves and drank our bit of water through the hollow reeds we carried round our necks.

"The stars are bright," said the shaman's son.

"Yes." I almost looked at the sky and brought rain, but I saw the look on his face and remembered just in time. From then on I turned Gian-nah-tah's words over in my mind as one turns over a rock to look for scorpions before handling it. Only when I was sure there was no hidden dart did I answer or obey.

Day after day we followed Broken Nose through the desert into strange country. We kept to the mountains and rocky crags, eyes alert for the dust sign that betrayed movement in the dry country. Then we saw it. Not the thin whirling pole of a dust devil, but a blanket of dust that hardly moved over the slow heavy wagons. The dust settled when the Mexicanos stopped for their afternoon sleep. Then it rose and re-formed when the wagons creaked slowly on. Without stopping for rest, I could have run farther than the Mexicanos traveled in one morning.

We watched them for two days. Then Broken Nose said, "It is the same as I saw before. Each morning and afternoon they move just so far. Tomorrow they will stop near a shallow arroyo during the day. We will wait there until they sleep."

"We should hunt this herd from two sides," said a warrior.

"These deer frighten easily," said another. "We must give them room to run."

The others laughed.

We waited. The wagon train camped for the night. I sat

away from the others. As I tore at the dried meat and sipped my small share of water through the reed, I watched the foolish Mexicanos make targets of themselves around the huge fires. How easy it would be to creep close and pick them off silently with the bow. But the night must be left peaceful for the spirits of the Old Ones.

When the Mexicanos had rolled into their striped blankets, Broken Nose led us on. He left Gian-nah-tah and me to hide in the long grass far up the side of a mesa. Though we were made to serve the warriors and do all the lowly camp work, we were sacred in our apprenticeship. We were under the care of Child-of-Water. If anything should happen to us, unspeakable evil would befall our band. So we were left in safety to learn through watching.

The warriors moved on to prepare the ambush. I was alone with the shaman's son.

There was no reason why we should not sleep. I curled up in the rough grass. The shaman's son sat with his knees gathered to his broad chest. The rising moon glinted in his open eyes. I caught my breath. I had seen that look before. The look of an animal stalking its prey; the look of a woman shrieking for revenge; the blood lust of a warrior in the war dance. I shivered, but I was not cold. Those gleaming eyes were fixed on me.

The life of an apprentice is sacred.

I did not know I had said it aloud until Gian-nah-tah said, "What makes you think that?"

I jumped. "It is true. Everyone knows it. The band that camped in the Canyon of the Falls lost an apprentice on a raid. A strange sickness spread among them, and most died. I have seen the survivors in Juan José's camp. Their faces are pitted with round scars."

He grinned wickedly. "And have you also seen those who have touched a rattlesnake running about without their skins?"

The thought that Lazy Legs had stirred leaped to my mind. It was true. There was no harm in touching a rattlesnake. Not unless it bit. And now that Gian-nah-tah had discovered one of the laws to be false, he was going to gamble that all others were untrue. The shaman's son was wrong. Just because a man told one lie, it did not follow that he never spoke the truth. But I did not argue with Gian-nah-tah. I felt in my medicine bag for the smooth blue stone. The night moved on. I clutched the turquoise and called upon its medicine to protect me from the thoughts that showed in those eyes. Eyes that never left me until the sky paled at the desert's edge.

I fitted my body into a hollow and pulled up grass to fill the spaces between the clumps on the low bank. There was not much danger of us being seen, but one can never be too careful. Gian-nah-tah did the same and stretched out beside me. I yawned and scolded myself for my fears of the night before. There was nothing but eagerness in his eyes this morning. I'd lost my sleep for nothing.

A spirit-carrying breeze pushed gently at my hair and whispered that I was wrong. There *had* been something in my companion's eyes. Something it would be well for me to remember in the future when I was no longer under the care of Child-of-Water.

The sun warmed my back. My eyes drooped. My head nodded. I must have slept, for a sharp jab of Gian-nah-tah's scratch stick brought me only half awake. I watched a line of ants march over the grass stems in front of me. I yawned again and forced my eyes wide.

During my training I had been forced to stay awake two days and two nights. It had been easier then with the drumming and chanting and activity of the camp. Here the buzz of insects and the chatter of birds were like my mother's lullaby. I pinched myself, but still my head nodded and my breathing deepened into sleep again and again. Then the squeal of cart wheels broke the desert sounds. Tense with excitement, I peered between the grass blades.

The dust cloud had been approaching while I fought sleep. The wagon train was almost below us. The heavy carts grated and groaned on their wooden wheels. Even without the dust every creature in the valley would be warned of their approach. I counted fourteen wagons, each with a driver. Four men on horseback guarded each side of the train. Two boys, far back, herded extra horses and mules. Only twenty-four Mexicanos to seven of our warriors.

I grinned at Gian-nah-tah. "Broken Nose spoke the truth," I said. "It will be easy."

He nodded and turned his gaze back to the wagons. He licked his lips, and I heard his breath coming short and hard.

All feeling for sleep left me as I watched the first wagon lurch past the arroyo where the warriors hid. I could see into the long shallow ditch. I knew the warriors were there. But they lay so still and blended so well into the earth and shadows that I could not make them out until the sun caught something bright. One quick flash of light. Then another.

Gian-nah-tah nudged me. "What is that?"

"The bracelet of Mexicano silver that Broken Nose wears on his upper arm."

He grunted. "No warrior in my raiding parties will wear silver."

I eased my legs under my body and rested my weight on toes and hands. If the Mexicanos saw the gleam and attacked, we would have to dash into the rocky crevices behind us. With no weapons for hunting or defending ourselves, we would have to hide until the warriors came to guide us home. If the warriors were killed, we would be left with nothing but our bare hands and our prayers.

The first horseman on the near side swung toward the arroyo. Had he seen the warriors? The first wagon followed him. Then the second wagon swung off in the other direction. I sighed and lay down. For days I had watched the Mexicanos turn their wagons into two lines headed back the way they'd come, forming a circle. I watched it again. And again I wondered why they did it. At first I thought it was for protection, but it could not be for that. If they were afraid of attack, why did they move with so much noise, send no scouts ahead or far to the sides and post their sentries where they could be seen against the big fires?

The animals were fed and watered. Again big fires were built. They lit the wasteful fires and cooked meals three times a day. If I had not seen it, I would never have believed it. How Lazy Legs' eyes would open when I told him!

Then I remembered that my brother had been born of these people. Perhaps, if my father had not rescued him, he would be with this train. One of the boy herders was built much like my brother. I heard him singing as he scattered the fire. He moved as Lazy Legs did, and the way he threw himself down in the shade to sleep was very like my brother's. How Lazy Legs would like that big black hat to shade his face while he slept! And the wide red band around the waist!

Gian-nah-tah sucked in his breath. While I'd been lost in thought, the warriors had wriggled over the rim of the arroyo and were within bowshot of the sleeping Mexicanos. Even the two men left on guard were nodding over their guns. As the warriors crept still closer, turning their heads to watch the others, I could see the ghost paint on their faces. They looked fierce enough to frighten the worst of devils.

My eyes turned to the one with the wide hat and the red sash. Some evil spirit took away my senses, for I suddenly believed Red Sash was my brother. My brother lying there waiting for death. My lips moved as I sent warning thoughts to wake him. Danger, I tried to tell him. Wake. There is danger.

The was scream beat against our ears. Arrows flew. Rifles cracked. And there were other screams. Screams of fear that brought me to myself. I yelled the war cry with Gian-nah-tah. Men ran from the wagons to the horses, cut their hobbles and swung to the bare backs.

"After them!" yelled Gian-nah-tah. "Kill them all!"

That one thought he was a war chief already. Anyone
with sense could see the stampeding animals were more important than a few cowardly Mexicanos. Though their front
legs were tied together, horses and mules were scattering
in all directions. The time of danger was past. I ran from
the hiding place and caught two mules and a gray-spotted
mare. I led them to Broken Nose, who was directing the

killing of the wounded. He motioned me onto the horse. I grabbed the gray mane and mounted. Broken Nose bent quickly and cut the hobbles.

He gave me no sign or order. Truly, I did not wait for any. My heels seemed to kick of themselves and my hands to pull the mane this way or that without any thought of mine. The mare obeyed quickly. I rode here and there, helping two warriors to herd together the frightened mules. We soon had them hopping together toward the wagons. They snorted and reared at the scent of blood. We rode round, calming them, and at last they began to graze fitfully. Only the mare I rode was not shivering. I slid to the ground. Calmly she bent to pull at a few strands of the brown grass. She lifted her head and blew through her nose holes when I walked away to the wagons. She was a good horse. Someone would get a prize when the loot was divided.

Gian-nah-tah was counting the dead. "There are only eighteen. I would not have let so many escape."

I glanced at the bodies. Before the raid an evil spirit had softened my heart with strange thoughts. That evil one was still with me. For when I saw Red Sash lying face down, his wide black hat on the ground beside him, I thought of my brother and was sick with fear. Broken Nose came up to strip the body of loot. He yanked at the red sash. The body rolled and I turned away, afraid to look at the face.

There was a shout. Warriors ran from one wagon to another, tearing at the coverings. The men waved their rifles at Broken Nose and yelled in anger. I moved closer, but it was some time before I understood the reason for their rage. All but two of the wagons carried nothing but strange machines. Some of them had seen such things at the town near Juan José's camp.

"Machines for digging the pesh and curing it!" shouted one man. "Only two wagons of any value!"

"Ey, what will my wives say?" moaned another. "Three of them with tongues sharp as thorns. I believe it is time I paid a long visit to my cousin in the Chiricahuas." He picked up his weapons and trotted off.

The warriors were still yelling. "Our shares will not be worth the time we spent and the risk we took."

"Have I eyes that see through wood?" shouted Broken Nose. "How was I to know what the wagons carried? When you see wagons traveling a great distance, isn't it safe to think they carry something of value?"

There was truth in that. The men grumbled, but decided to make the best of it. With mules and ropes they over-turned the wagons and spilled the worthless machines onto the sand. Then we loaded mules with all the clothing, guns, ammunition and food we could find. I kicked the wide hat Red Sash had worn under the hoofs of the mules. After that, no one wanted it, and I was glad. I did not want to be reminded of my weakness.

We took the homeward trail. Gian-nah-tah and I trailed behind, herding the extra mules. Gian-nah-tah sat a wobbly horse whose coat looked as ragged as my father's old buffalo robe. I rode the gray-spotted mare. No one had said I could, but no one had protested when I caught her up before anyone had mounted.

The shaman's son scowled and mumbled under his breath the whole way. He never put words to his thoughts, but I read them just the same. With so little loot, he was thinking, the apprentices would be lucky to get a bit of cloth for a headband. He was not the only one. The men complained openly every night when we camped.

"Better for us to have stayed in camp to hunt," they said. "This trifle will be gone in no time. We shall have to risk our lives a second time to get what we were promised by a blind scout with a crooked nose."

I kept my mind on my duties and tried not to look too happy. Not one of us had been scratched. There would be no mourning in camp. Though the loot was small, it had been a victory. Most important of all, I had taken my first big step toward manhood and I had served without shaming my father. So I followed in the warriors' dust, riding the good gray horse and listening to the song of joy in my heart.

The women did not welcome us into camp. Broken Nose did not dare to send a warrior ahead, as was the custom. He knew the man would voice complaints instead of announcing a victory. As leader, he could not do it himself. It would not be modest. More than once I saw him glance at me, but announcing victory was a warrior's privilege. So we rode into camp behind the sentry's signal and everyone was too surprised to notice how few of the mules carried packs.

They ran to cheer us. I made the mare dance so that I could look for my family while I seemed only to be calming a nervous horse. The women were there, holding the

Little One up to see. The young boys crowded close to touch the horses and ask questions. My brother's smiling face was not among them. I looked about openly, not caring if anyone saw. For I thought of Red Sash and a pain I had never felt before tore through my heart. When I saw him coming at a fast walk, the pain left. Anger took its place. Then shame bowed my head. Shame at my thoughts of the Mexicano. Was there no way to rid myself of this spirit that weakened my heart and mind?

Broken Nose pointed out three mules for the women to cook for the feast. I reached down and cut one of the silver circles from the decorated saddle. Then I slid to the ground and patted the horse. When I turned regretfully away, there was Little One with her begging eyes. I pulled her finger from her mouth and pressed the bit of silver into her hand. She smiled and ran to show her mother.

Lazy Legs touched my arm. "Come away from this noise and tell me all about it."

My tongue held bitter words about his slowness in meeting us, but bitter words withered quickly under my brother's smile. Then it came to me that he might know something of the strange thoughts I'd had. He had so many of them himself.

"Where can we go that no one will follow?" I asked.

"The little cave where I waited when you hunted the ducks." He frowned. "It's a long way."

"I have been farther for less. Let us go."

I set him a fast pace. It was good to work my legs after so many days on a horse. We squeezed inside the small cave and settled for talk. Lazy Legs pulled a pouch from a ledge and offered me a strip of dried meat.

"There is still some left?"

He grinned. "I'm not often hungry enough to come this far. Eat and we will talk."

He ate. I talked. Though when I told of my thoughts on the Mexicano with the red sash, his jaws forgot to move. He stared at me until I finished. Then he chewed slowly and swallowed. Still he said nothing. I grew angry at having told him.

"But it is really nothing," I said. "I will ask the shaman for a charm and all will be well."

"No."

"You mean a charm is not enough?"

He shook his head. "I mean you should not tell the shaman."

My mouth fell open. Of all his strange thoughts, this was the strangest. "The shaman must be told everything. How else can one be cured?"

"Perhaps you are not sick."

"I didn't say I was sick. I said an evil spirit possessed me."

"How do you know it was evil?"

"Because it put thoughts into my head that no warrior ever has." I ducked out of the cave and stood upright. "I am of the People and we are not weak."

I strode away, not caring if he followed or stayed to stuff himself until he was too fat to get out of the cave. I would go to the shaman. I would get a charm and be safe from this weakness that might keep me from becoming a warrior.

My steps hurried. Yes, this was a dangerous thing. Better for the legs to fail at running or the wrist to weaken on the bow than to have a heart soft toward the enemy. I must see the shaman before this sickness destroyed my manhood.

EIGHT

A SHARE
OF
THE SPOILS

My path to the shaman led through the village. A group of young boys were gathered near my father's wickiups, craning their necks and buzzing like bees around a cactus blossom. I joined them, curious to see what caused so much excitement. When I peered over their heads, I was just as awed as they. A visitor sat by my father's fire. Even without the red shirt I would have known my cousin by his massive head and shoulders.

My father saw me and motioned for me to join them. The boys moved back to make a path for me as if I were a great chief. Proudly I stepped forward and sat across from the men. The boys continued to whisper and giggle until Lazy Legs' mother came out and shooed them away.

Mangas studied me, his eyes twinkling. "I heard you were hunting two-legged deer and part of the herd escaped."

I glanced at my father. He shook his head. "I did not tell him. He knew when he arrived."

"The men who escaped rode until their horses dropped beneath them," said Mangas. "They were not far from the safe trail. It was not long until they were found and riders sent to the town with the news of the attack."

Slowed by the herd and sure we were not followed, we had not hurried. The news could easily have reached the Mexicanos before we were halfway home.

"Some of our people were visiting in the Mexicano town." Mangas glanced at my father and explained, "It is a good way to hear the news. They all slipped away quickly, for the Mexicanos were angry. They were also very frightened. The sentries they put out shot at shadows. All night long . . . bang! . . . bang!" He laughed hard. "With so many bullets flying, it is a wonder they did not shoot each other. Not one of us was near the town. Such a waste of ammunition."

He became serious again. "The next day they came and talked with our chief. They were very angry. They said we have no right to raid their ranches and wagon trains when we have made peace."

"They lie," said my father. "We made no peace. Juan José promised them safety in their town and on the two safe trails. That is all. The promise has been kept."

"That is what our chief told them."

"One town and two trails are not enough for them. They want it all."

"If they do, they have said nothing about it."

My father frowned. "It is not like them. Didn't they make any demands?"

"Yes, but you will never guess what they were. They wanted our warriors to go with them to load the machines on the wagons and bury their dead. Juan José told them that his warriors had not made the raid and he knew nothing of it. Besides, his warriors had their own work to do. That made the Mexicanos angrier, for they knew what sort of work he meant."

"But there was no fighting?"

Mangas shook his head. "There were too many of us. We can destroy them, and they know it."

There was silence as they filled their pipes and lit them with a stick from the small fire. My father had invited me to sit that I might listen and learn. I had no right to speak unless spoken to, but I longed to ask questions. It seemed to me that the Mexicanos were overly excited about a raid that had been so disappointing to us. Especially since it did not violate the terms of the treaty. Then Mangas spoke again, so softly I leaned forward to catch the words.

"The last time we met, you gave me words to hold close and ponder on."

My father nodded. "I remember."

"I was asleep. Your words awakened me. I saw the Mexicanos coming in great numbers. They bring their women and children. Soon they will outnumber us. Will they fear us then? Or will the thought of losing their families be enough to keep the peace?"

"They have not the courage to attack us."

"Not alone, but the trader Johnson and other white-eyes have been whispering among them. We cannot discover what they say, but suspicion and unrest follow their talks. Who knows what they are promising? I will speak true, cousin. I fear for our people."

"It is too late. The agreement is made. We cannot break it."

"That is true. But I have thought of a plan. What if we should tell them of a place where there is more pesh in the ground? A place far away from us. Perhaps they would go to find it and we would be rid of them without trouble."

My father stared thoughtfully at the fire. "I do not think they will believe us." He raised his hand to silence our cousin's protest. "But if it seems that the Mexicanos are about to break the treaty, I will counsel Juan José to try your plan."

The council fire blazed. The drums beat. Broken Nose cried, "Hear me! We have killed many enemies!" There was an answering shout from the women. The victory feast had begun.

I leaped to my feet and ran to watch the sharing of the spoils. Broken Nose named each man, and the warrior stepped forward to receive his share. Often I had watched my father divide the spoils, and always he was generous. Of course, Broken Nose hadn't much to share. After the warriors came the widows and the old ones. My mind ran rapidly over the amount already given. Broken Nose would have less than anyone. I stood straight, proud to have served with such a generous man.

"Killer-of-Death."

I stepped forward, expecting a bit of cloth or corn that I could give the women.

"Killer-of-Death was greater than an apprentice," said Broken Nose. "He moved quickly and without command to save the mules and horses. He will be a man among men. For such as he I have saved the gray-spotted mare."

My feet took root. I could not believe what I heard. Some of the warriors had received little more. And to be praised before the whole village and my cousin Mangas Colorado was more honor than I deserved.

Broken Nose turned away and called, "Gian-nah-tah!"

My feet moved then. I went to find the gray mare and lead her to my father's herd. She nuzzled my shoulder. I seized her mane to lead her, for the bridle and saddle had been given to someone else. She tossed her head and whinnied. Startled, I moved away. She stepped toward me. I walked backward and saw there was no need to lead her. She followed me like the Little One.

I led her across the stream to my father's horses. For the first time I saw the usefulness of the closed-in places the Mexicanos made to keep their horses. What did it matter if a few horses strayed to the mountains? My father had more than thirty. But I had only one. I could not chance losing her. As I stood there, I remembered Lazy Legs' dog.

My brother had once taken a liking to a puppy and treated it with as much affection as a mother gave her child. Everyone had laughed at him for taking such trouble with a dog, but the puppy had followed Lazy Legs everywhere. It slept at his feet, and if it strayed, my brother's whistle always brought it to his side. Until that day when it was found with an arrow through its heart. Had it been Gian-nah-tah's, as Lazy Legs had claimed?

I remembered and wondered if the same kindness would keep the mare close to me. She already had a liking for me. I whistled softly between my teeth and tugged her mane. She followed, but only because I led the way. With training, I hoped she would learn to obey the whistle only. I twisted hobbling thongs between her forelegs and pulled grass for her to eat. Tomorrow, when I began to train her, I would bring corn.

From the sounds at the fire I knew the victory dance was over and the feasting begun. I hurried back, hungry and happy. As I pushed my way toward my family, the shaman's son blocked my path. In his hand was his share of the spoils. The red sash. I stared at the red cloth, then up at his flashing eyes. Without a word he leaned forward and spat at my moccasins. Then he turned away, his broad back rigid with anger.

I was curled under my blanket before I remembered that I had not seen the shaman. But no matter. There was plenty of time, and it no longer seemed so urgent.

Mangas stayed on for three days. He played hoop-and-pole with the men, hunted for food for the cookpots and silently watched me work with the mare.

She learned quickly to answer the pressures of my knees
and toes. When the time came, I would be able to guide her
and have both hands free to shoot. She was slower in learning to answer the whistle. Sometimes she obeyed. Other
times she ignored me. Mangas laughed and said it was because she was a woman. Lazy Legs came often to watch,
and many times I caught a glimpse of Shy Maiden standing quietly nearby, her soft eyes following my every movement. Then I would leap on the mare and make her rear
and dance.

Mangas caught me at it once. "One woman at a time," he

told me and laughed harder than ever. "Or are you truly training that horse for your father-in-law to ride?"

I blushed. After that, I pretended not to see Shy Maiden even when Lazy Legs whispered that she was there.

On the last day of our cousin's visit my father called me to him.

"Mangas is leading a raid on a large ranch. He has asked warriors from our camp to join."

My heart thumped. Did I dare ask to serve with such a great man?

"He has heard Broken Nose. He believes you will bring luck."

I didn't wait to hear more. "I will go."

He nodded. "Our warriors are to meet him at a place they know, but you will leave with Mangas today and remain in his care."

My anger at being treated like a child must have shown in my face, for my father rested his hand on my shoulder. "I want you to see the Mexicano town. Use your eyes well. Forget nothing and think long on what you see."

"I will remember."

He paused as if he would say more, but he only looked at me for a moment in a strange way. Then he walked toward the shaman's wickiup.

I hurried to prepare for the journey and the raid that would follow. Lazy Legs helped to put the small rawhide saddle on my horse. When I mounted, he grasped my ankle.

"Be careful. Last night our father had a dream."

"Do you know what it told?"

Lazy Legs shook his head. "But it could not have been a good sign. He was worried all this morning. I heard him tell my mother that he had to speak to you before you left."

"He said nothing about a dream or sign."

"Perhaps I am wrong. But take care. Come back to us."

"Never fear, I will make a runner of you yet."

I rode off, sure that nothing evil could befall me. It was well known that Mangas Colorado never gambled with his life, never risked an attack unless sure he would come safely through. Red Sleeves' raids were always successful and as safe as a hunting party. Besides, what could happen to an apprentice who was always left in safety?

I smiled. As always, Lazy Legs was making much of nothing. My father's dream could not have been of me.

NINE

THE ENEMY
STRIKES

The unshod hoofs thumped softly over the ground. We kept to the hills and did not hurry. Indeed, we could have traveled as fast on foot, but men from my father's camp and one other were to meet at a place all warriors knew, and Mangas wished to arrive last.

As we rode I thought of what I had seen in the Mexicano town. Mostly I remembered the noise. Shouting and singing barely heard over the pounding and thumping of machines and tools. Even in the short silences there were the rattle of harness and the clanking of great round spurs. They were building a great many places to live. It did not seem to me that the Mexicanos planned to move for a long time. Nor did I think Mangas' plan to tell them of more pesh would make them stir. Not when so many were settling their families in wickiups that took so much trouble to build and could not be moved.

The things I had seen in Juan José's camp disturbed me more. I could not help but notice how little game went into the cookpots. Most of the food was from the Mexicano village. Game was scarce, the men had said. What did they expect with all the noise? I shook my head sadly. If I were chief, I would move the people into the mountains before the men forgot how to hunt and the women lost their energy for gathering food. But I was not chief. I was on my second raid, eager to have it past so that my last one as an apprentice would be at hand.

We reached the meeting place. As soon as I slid from my horse, I saw the moccasin print. The heel had been set down hard. I searched among the warriors from my father's camp. As I thought, the shaman's son was among them. I would have to be even more careful of my duties. Gian-nah-tah was a warrior now. I did not want to give him anything to say against me when we returned.

We traveled steadily into strange country with rolling mountains separated by dry rivers. With so little level land, more scouts were sent out around us. At last Mangas led us up a mountain and into the shadow of a jagged cliff. Below us, in the level space between the mountains, spread the ranch. The closed-in places were crowded with horses and mules. Many cattle bobbed along the riverbed to the dark wet places. Men moved out of the shadows of the buildings.

"Soldiers," said a warrior.

"How many?" asked another.

"Three times our number," said Mangas. "They have been sent to find us. Or others of our People."

I waited for the men to turn their horses toward home, as they often did when they considered a raid too dangerous. But there was not even a murmur. It was then that I knew how great was their respect for Mangas Colorado. When I heard his plan, I knew also the greatness of my cousin's mind.

The soldiers at the ranch were looking for our warriors. It was Red Sleeves' plan to let them find us. Seven warriors would creep round the ranch and attack on foot at first light. Using all the tricks of dodging and concealment, they would keep just out of range of the soldiers' guns. When the army was far into the hills and the horses tired, the warriors were to slip away and join us on the homeward trail. While the seven men led the soldiers a lively chase, Mangas and the rest would attack the ranch. The few people left there would surrender quickly or try to escape.

I thought it an excellent plan except for one thing. I was to be left behind to tend the horses of the first seven warriors. It was my duty as an apprentice, but from the hiding place I would see nothing of the raid.

There was praying that night, and hoddentin floated

thick on the cooling air. Seven warriors applied the ghost paint that protected in battle. Then they slipped into the dark. Much later the cry of a coyote sounded from beyond the ranch. Mangas answered. All was ready.

Dawn came with the screech of war whoops and a burst of gunfire. The bawling of frenzied horses and frightened men drifted faintly to us. More gunfire, then scattered hoofbeats gathered to a thunder that rolled away in the distance. Silence hung over the mountains. Mangas sat motionless on his horse. Suddenly he kicked his horse around and down the hill. The warriors plunged after him. In two breaths I was alone with the echoes of their yells.

I longed to call my horse and ride to the cliff and watch, but I had been ordered to stay. I kicked at a red boulder, paced to a thorn bush and back to the boulder. The horses rolled their eyes and tossed their heads, sensing my nervousness. I sat on the boulder and tried to act calm. But who could ignore the battle sounds that found their way to the camp?

Hoofbeats! I jumped to my feet. Was it a soldier? I had no weapons. Listening closely, I knew I was safe. The hoofs were unshod. Gian-nah-tah galloped into the hollow.

"Get a horse and follow me!" he shouted.

"Why?"

"The soldiers returned and are fighting this way. Mangas sent me to take you to safety."

I whistled, but the gray mare chose not to answer.

"Hurry!" Gian-nah-tah called.

I grabbed the nearest horse, a brown stallion with a bad temper, and followed the shaman's son. I gave no thought to the horses I was tending. The safety of an apprentice is worth more than horses. The thought that rode with me was that neither of my raids had been a success. Perhaps the gods did not favor me or some evil spirit shadowed my manhood.

Gian-nah-tah whirled his horse. I tried to follow, but

the stallion refused. When I hauled back on the rein, he reared and turned on his hind legs. As he spun, I caught the glint of sun on the throwing ax raised in Gian-nah-tah's hand. I slipped sideways, but was too slow. The ax struck my head and I fell down . . . down . . . into nothing.

 TEN

"APACHE!"

The dark shadows moved silently across the sunset, the only sounds the clink of metal and the creak of leather. Three were held in their saddles by companions. One was carried in a litter. Grit from the shod hoofs flew near enough to strike my outstretched hand. I lay still, hardly breathing. With bowed heads they passed by without a glance at where I lay.

What did it mean? Were these the soldiers who had chased the first small group of warriors? Gian-nah-tah had said they'd returned, that the raid was broken.

I sat up and clenched my teeth against the pain in my head. I touched the wound and felt sand dried hard in the blood. Gian-nah-tah was a liar. And it was only by luck he was not a murderer. If the stallion hadn't reared, the throwing ax would have split my head like a ripe gourd. As it was, I had lost blood. Weak and far from home without weapons, I might yet join the Old Ones.

Why? Why? The question beat in my head with every stab of pain. Why had he tricked me into following him? Why had he tried to kill me? True, I had tried to kill him with the snakeskin, but that was nearly a harvest past. If he wanted vengeance for that, he should have challenged me when I returned from the dry country.

Gently at first, I tried my arms and legs. I was bruised and sore, but nothing was broken. Child-of-Water must have protected me in my fall. I rose unsteadily to my feet.

I was of the People. I was strong and hard. I would live and have vengeance. This I promised.

But vengeance would have to wait. I glanced around with no sense of where our mountains were. A flame rose in the darkness. The soldiers had camped, but they would return to the ranch. I had only to follow them, then take the trail of the raiders. Food and water were a problem. But hadn't I found them during my fourteen days in the desert?

I fingered the wound on my head. If it healed, all would be well. But without a shaman to care for it, I might become sick or worse. I turned my thoughts away. That was in the hands of the gods. I would do all I could. Usen and Child-of-Water must decide the rest.

The soldiers' camp was not like that of the wagon train. Here there was no laughter, no singing. Sentries were posted well out, but they did not bother to hide themselves. Even when they squatted on their heels, they were clearly seen against the firelight. Creeping between them was easier than stalking a deer. I lay hidden until the soldiers gathered around the food.

Carefully I snaked to the litter, for next to the wounded soldier lay a water bag. Even if it were empty, I would need it when I found water. The man groaned, but I had nothing to fear. A bullet had found his heart's place. I could see from his face that he would die. Clutching the water bag, I wriggled backward. Two soldiers came to the dying man. I lay still, for any movement would betray me.

I could not make out what the soldiers carried or what they did. The dying man screamed once and was silent. Had they killed the man on the litter so they could move faster? They were not being pursued. No, there was no reason for killing the wounded man. It looked as though the soldier kneeling by the litter used a knife. Did they torture their own kind? The other soldier held out a small pan, and the knife soldier dropped something into it with a clang. They had removed the bullet from the wounded man!

Could such a thing be done so close to the heart? Surely the knife soldier did not have medicine strong enough for that.

Water sloshed in the bag. Safely past the sentries, I sipped it and thought on what I had seen. No, it could not be. I

had seen death on that man's face. They would bury him at dawn. But at dawn the man drank from a water bag, and the next day, before we reached the ranch, the knife soldier fed him. Truly, the Mexicanos had strong medicine. Had Juan José chosen the wrong gods, after all? Such thoughts were too great for me. I put them aside for more important things.

I circled the ranch and the place where Mangas had made camp. The homeward trail lay clear before me, and, from what I read, the raid had been a great victory with many horses and cattle for everyone. But one less son in my father's wickiups.

I wondered what sort of tale Gian-nah-tah had told. Surely it had been one that would convince Mangas there was no use sending a warrior back to search for me. I only hoped his story did not shame me. That would be too much for my father to bear.

That night the Thunder People shook the earth. I piled rocks and dirt into curved walls against the hillside to catch the rain and fill the water bag. I was overjoyed with the gift of water until I rose with the sun to take the trail. There was no trail. The rain that had filled the water bag and cut ridges in the mountainside had also washed away all signs of the raiding party.

I trotted in ever wider circles, up the mountains and in the clefts between, but I found no sign. Every brush-covered mountain was as rounded and unmarked as the next. Each riverbed was the same as any other. No jagged peaks, no animal-shaped crags, no landmarks of any kind. There was but one thing to do. Keep the sun to my right in the beginning of the day and to my left when it began its downward sweep. And move on. On and on and on.

At first I burned from inside and the country moved like water before my eyes. It cleared when my head wound ceased its throbbing, but I had used more water than I should have. The water bag was almost empty. The fever had weakened my legs. I could not have run down game if I had seen any. Nor could I hunt, for I had no weapons. I picked half-ripened cactus fruit, tearing my hands on the spines in my eagerness for the juicy food. Long dry pods hung on the mesquite trees, but the beans were small and I wasted time cracking them between stones to make them soft enough to eat.

I do not know how many days I traveled before the hills dropped away to wide desert broken by rocky crags. And beyond, at the rim of the sky, rose our mountains. Home!

My legs moved of their own accord. Straight into the desert I ran and jumped and shouted. And of their own accord my legs folded under me and I fell to the sand. I picked myself up and trudged slowly on, eyes watering and blinking against the glare.

Home and the village. How pleased they'd be to see me. All except the shaman's son. Should I challenge him to fight hand-to-hand, as Mangas had fought his brothers-in-law? Or should I stand before the council and denounce him as a liar and a murderer? I smiled as I thought of what would happen.

Then I stopped and stared at the moccasin print before me. Faint and shuffling, but a track. I blinked stupidly and looked up. The mountains were no nearer. Unsteadily I lifted one foot and placed it in the print. It fitted. Tears blurred my vision. How long had I walked in a dream,

staring at the ground before me? How much of the day had I wasted by walking in a circle? I swayed on my aching legs. My mind was too weary for thought. I would sit here and rest. Rest . . . but something inside warned me to go on.

On to the crag ahead where a dark line meant trees. Mesquite trees with hard dry beans and perhaps a pool of water. My mind stirred enough to tell me that if I stayed here to rest, I would never move again. I forced my feet to move. One foot, then the other. Over and over. I stumbled and fell. The sand burned my chest and face, but how good it was to lie down!

Get up, said the voice inside me. Get up or you will never see your home.

I drank the last of the water, pushed myself to my feet and moved on. On to the trees. Green-barked trees. When I was close enough to see they'd put out their long string leaves, I knew water had run recently in the riverbed. Very recently, for the sandy bottom was a darker shade than the earth I stood on. I slid down the steep bank and scooped a hole in the damp earth. Then, holding my tattered breechcloth away from my body, I filled it with the dry pods from the overhanging branches. They were smaller than mesquite beans. Even full, my breechcloth would not hold enough to fill my stomach.

Water had seeped into the hole. I sat beside it, sipping the water through the drinking reed and shelling beans until long after dark. Then I crawled out of the riverbed and under the drooping tree branches and slept.

As always, the Little One had awakened first. She stood staring down at me in the dim light of the wickiup. I reached up drowsily, pulled her thumb from her mouth and turned over for more sleep. Something pressed hard against my arm. I pushed it away, but it did not move. I ran my hand over it. What was a tree trunk doing inside the wickiup? My eyes followed it up to the drooping green branches. I remembered the night before and sighed. It was only the little girl who'd made me think I was home.

Girl! Wide awake, I sprang to my feet. She was still there, staring round-eyed over the thumb that was back in her mouth. She was younger than my sister and not so chubby. Her only clothing was a charm of some sort around her neck. She was not of the People. That I knew. I swallowed hard. I must be in Papago country. She was one of the Bean People.

I peered through the branches, but saw no one. There was no danger yet. And there would be none if I did as any warrior would do. Grab her by the heels and whirl her head against the tree trunk. My mouth went dry. She was so small. So much like the Little One as she stood there with her thumb in her mouth. But this was no time for weakness. She was danger. She was an enemy. She must be destroyed.

I moved toward her. She skipped from under the tree and waited for me, smiling and holding out a strange toy. That was good. She had no fear of me, and I must do it quickly before someone came to look for her. She shook the toy impatiently, her eyes like the Little One's when she brought me the cradleboard to tie. Slowly, so as not to frighten her into screaming, I reached forward. My hand closed on the toy, a stick with rings and a thong. She laughed and clapped her hands.

"Apache!" A woman ran toward us. "Apache!" she screamed again.

As if by magic, two warriors appeared and whipped arrows to their bows. I grabbed the little girl and held her to my chest as a shield. The woman yelled to the men. They lowered their bows and looked from us to the woman. Holding the girl with both arms, I backed toward a rocky crag behind me.

ELEVEN

VENGEANCE

A fine bag of bones! I huddled on the ledge, turning them over in my mind. First, there were the Papago men prowling in the darkness below, their arrows thirsty for my blood. The woman was most likely urging them on, as women do. But the girl was the sharpest bone of all. Why hadn't I killed her when I had the chance? Why had I waited that one little time that made it too late?

It was the same spirit that had been in me when I watched the wagon train and the boy who reminded me of my brother. This time it had cast the spell of the Little

One over me. Why hadn't I told the shaman and received a charm to make me hard as a warrior should be? Was I to spend my life weakened by the thought that this enemy was like Lazy Legs and that one like my sister and another like my father or cousin? A sorry warrior I would make. Better to stay in camp and help the women grind corn and carry water. I sighed and turned my thoughts to escaping the Bean People.

Apache! the woman had screamed. Their word for enemy. But they were the enemy, not I. I did not want their child. I had trouble enough taking care of myself.

I glanced at the girl curled beside me. In the moonlight she looked very much like my sister. Not as pretty, but just as brave. She had gone to sleep without a whimper for food or water.

As I waited for the moon to reach the end of its sky trail, I thought on the girl beside me and her mother watching and waiting below. How like my mother she was in her fear for the life of her little one. The warriors also had held their arrows to save the child, as any of the People would have done. I thought of the Mexicano on the wagon train and of Lazy Legs, born of the Mexicano but so much of the People. The girl also was very like the People. Then came a strange thought. If the Papago and the Mexicanos were so much like the People, what made them enemies?

Ey, foolish thoughts! Thoughts so weak even a woman would blush to carry them in her head. Angrily I stood and made my way along the ledge.

Before the moonlight had faded, I had seen a place where I could climb over the jagged peak. Once down the other side, I could move far across the desert before first light. The girl was in no danger. When dawn came and I threw no more rocks from the ledge, her people would climb up and find her.

The far side of the peak sloped steeply to the desert. I stumbled down, bouncing from one boulder to another. The Thunder People were busy over our mountains. I smiled. The rain would gather in the arroyos, giving me water, and the lightning would guide me through the night. Usen was good.

All day I kept watch, but the girl's people did not pursue me. The black clouds rolled off the mountains, bringing rain to the desert. Water was everywhere. By throwing stones, I chased a coyote from its kill. The mangled rabbit strengthened my legs enough for me to run down a quail. After that, my journey was easier.

It was many days before I reached the mountains, and my moccasins wore through before I found a canyon I knew. A canyon two days' journey from camp, if the camp had not been moved since I left . . . how long ago? Long enough for the nights to turn cold and chill the bones. Long enough for the rains to have filled every stream to its brim. Teeth chattering from the night air and the cold water, I splashed eagerly through the stream beside the camp.

Cookfires glowed in the darkness. The scent of burning wood mingled with that of food and people. A baby cried

and was hushed. My throat tightened at the high thin laughter of old men and the yapping of dogs. Home! I was home, my cracked bleeding feet no longer pained. With firm step I entered the village.

The first one to see me screeched the news to the camp. They were all about me then, but staring at me in silence with no welcome in their faces. What had happened? Where were the warriors and their wives and the children? My mother pushed aside the old people and clutched me to her as if I were an infant. Lazy Legs' mother was there, too, crying and touching me tenderly. Between them, they washed my hair with their tears. I pulled away and led them to our wickiups, where my father stood waiting, his weathered cheeks wet in the firelight. He placed his hands on my shoulders and looked long into my eyes.

"The dream showed the truth," he said at last. "The boy has gone and will never return. But I did not understand. I thought never to see you again." His fingers gripped tightly.

"Brother!" A brown figure tore aside the blanket of the wickiup and charged into me. Down we went, a tangle of bony arms and legs. Lazy Legs sat astride me, his blue eyes laughing down at mine. "You came back!" He bounced happily on my chest. "What great deeds have you done? Tell me."

I poked the ribs showing clearly in his chest. He was as thin and lean as myself.

"Can this bag of bones be my brother?" I asked.

My father laughed. "His stomach was so filled with sorrow there was no room for food."

"It was not sorrow that kept me from eating," said my brother. "Why should I mourn for someone who pulls me from my sleep and forces me to run about the desert like a crazy rabbit? It was only that my taste for food left me." He raised his head and sniffed. "Ah, do I smell onions and mescal and fresh corn cakes?"

"You said you had no taste for food."

"I don't, but I shall force myself to eat. Now that my brother has returned, I shall have to strengthen my legs." He grinned, bounced hard enough to make me grunt and rolled off.

The Little One crept into my lap and clasped her arms around my neck. I thought of the Papago girl and how close she had come to death. I squeezed the Little One, glad she would always be safe. I looked around at my family and sighed.

"It is good to be among my people," I said.

A sudden hush fell over them. Lazy Legs opened his mouth, but my father spoke quickly.

"Eat and then we will talk."

The women had not cut their hair. Whatever Gian-nah-tah had told them, it was not that I had been killed. Where was the shaman's son? And the others missing from the camp? My father explained as I shared the hot food with Lazy Legs.

The white-eye trader Johnson had become a good friend to Juan José. To show his friendship, he had invited all of the People to a· feast now that his trading wagons had arrived.

"The wagons are said to be filled with gifts for all who attend the feast," said my father. "Two days ago our people left for Juan José's camp. All except the shaman and the ones too old to travel."

"Why didn't the shaman go?"

"The spirits have warned him that friendship with the white-eyes will bring disaster."

"And still our people went?"

He smiled. "Cookpots, knives and blankets make a shaman's voice difficult to hear. If our hearts had not been too heavy for feasting, we would have gone also."

Keeping my voice flat, I asked, "And the shaman's son?"

"He is a warrior now. He follows his own trail."

"He is here?"

"No, he went with Broken Nose to the feast." He filled his pipe and ordered the others to their blankets. "It is time for us to talk."

Lazy Legs grinned at me as he ducked into the wickiup. Many were the times we had lain silent behind the blankets to hear the warriors around the fire. Tonight I knew the women would also crouch there to hear my story. Perhaps it was a foolish custom, but one must show his manhood in some way.

My father lit his pipe, offered it to the Four Directions, then said, "Begin."

I began with the day, so long ago, when I had laid the deer track that led Gian-nah-tah to a skunk. Then the duck hunt, the rattlesnake and his threat on my first raid. I told it all, except for my moments of weakness. When I finished the story of my journey home, the pipe lay cold in my father's hand. He turned it over and over. At last he spoke.

"The shaman's son said that you ran from the raid."

"The shaman's son is a lying coyote."

His look silenced me. "The shaman's son said that he rode after you. When he caught your horse, you were trembling from fear. He laughed at you, saying that was not the way of warriors. Then you told him you would never be a warrior. That the ways of the People sickened you. The ways of the Mexicanos were better. You were going to make your home with them and they would be your people."

Now I understood the angry silence when I arrived. Anger burned hot within me, its red flames leaping up to color my vision. "I spoke the truth. Gian-nah-tah lies."

"So I thought. So I believe. But others . . ."

"What of the others?"

"They say your heart is soft. That you belong with the Mexicanos if you run at the sound of a war whoop."

"Enough!" The red flames blinded me. My hands reached for something to smash, found nothing and beat in rage at my legs. "I cannot live with this shame. I must have vengeance."

"That is true."

"I will challenge Gian-nah-tah and I will kill him." In that moment I could have done so. But the shaman's son was far away and it is easier to carry water in your two hands than to hold a killing anger in your heart.

"I must talk with the shaman," said my father.

As I waited for his return, I thought how it would be. How Gian-nah-tah and I would face each other with drawn knives. Knives that could be put away only when one of us was dead. This would be no enemy who faced me, but one I had run and feasted with. One with whom I had feathered arrows and trained for manhood. Even to save my honor, could I plunge my knife into the chest of one I knew like a brother? Twice my heart had softened for a strange enemy. How, then, could it harden toward Gian-nah-tah?

I jumped at my father's voice.

"My son, I have talked with the shaman. He said you cannot make the challenge. His son is a warrior. You are not."

"He wishes only to save his son."

My father turned quickly away. "Tomorrow we go to Juan José. He will decide."

Perhaps I would not have to fight Gian-nah-tah. I breathed easier at the thought. But my shame was like a splinter, jabbing and hurting when I least expected. Mixed with all the feelings was my fear of the spirit I carried within me.

The shaman and his wife traveled with us, but I dared not ask him for a charm. I nudged my horse close to my brother's, eager for something else to think on.

"What has happened since I left?"

"The one with many wives returned from his visit in the Chiricahuas."

"I meant something important."

Lazy Legs paid no attention, but went on with his story. "He brought a strange tale with him. The white-eyes are in the Chiricahuas."

"They are everywhere now, worse than the Mexicanos."

"But you will never guess what they are doing in the Chiricahuas. They are drawing a magic line on the ground."

"What kind of magic line?"

"I am not sure. The one with many wives says you cannot see it, but the white-eyes say it is there. The white-eyes also say all the country south of the line belongs to the Mexicanos and all the country on this side belongs to them."

I pulled my horse to a stop. "How can that be?"

"The white-eyes say they bought it from the Mexicanos."

"How could they sell what they did not own? All of the land belongs to the People."

"The Mexicanos say they have owned this land since before Juan José was born."

I laughed. "Is that what they call owning the land? Building a few ranches and towns for us to raid? Then we have nothing to worry about. Things will go on as before."

"I do not think so." He glanced sideways at me. "You will not believe this, brother."

"Tell me."

"The white-eyes say we are not to cross the line."

I frowned. "Does the line kill anyone who crosses?"

"No, for our cousins in the Chiricahuas have crossed it many times. But the white-eyes say when they bought the land they promised the Mexicanos that we would leave their towns and ranches in peace."

"Then how are we to live?"

"That they did not say."

"Let the white-eyes draw all the magic lines they want. Let them make treaties and say whatever foolishness comes into their heads. This country belongs to the People, and nothing they say or do will change it."

Lazy Legs began to argue, but I kicked my heels and galloped away from his gloomy looks. But the laughter soon passed and my worries once again shared my saddle. When we made camp that night, I rolled my blanket next to Lazy Legs' and told him of my worry.

"The last time I told you of this weakness," I said, "you did not think it was an evil spirit or a sickness. What do you think now?"

"I think the same."

"Then I can never be a warrior."

Lazy Legs raised himself on his arm. "That is not true.

Mangas is the greatest of warriors, but still he says the country is large enough for all. And he likes the white-eyes even though he does break into their stores now and then. Juan José is our greatest war chief, yet he welcomed the Mexicanos, and the trader Johnson visits often in his camp."

I turned it over in my mind. "How can one have the heart of a warrior and also have a soft heart for an enemy?"

"I do not know. Go to sleep."

"I cannot sleep."

He sighed. "Our father is still by the fire. Go ask him."

"No." What would he think of me asking such a question? But the worry would not let me rest. I threw aside the blanket and went to sit by the fire. We spoke of the signs along the trail, the joy of the women at attending the feast and what I had seen in the Mexicano town.

Then I said, "Juan José was a great warrior. Why does he now give friendship to the enemy? Isn't that a sign of weakness?"

"Not when a man has proved a strong heart. When a prisoner is tortured, many men walk away so as not to see. No one thinks them weak if they have fought well."

I lowered my head. "What if one has such feelings before he has proved himself?"

"When I was a boy, there was a man in our camp who never joined a raid or a war party. The signs, he said, were always bad. He had heard an owl outside his wickiup or a dream had told him there would soon be a great need for arrowheads and he must stay at home and chip them. When lions or grizzlies roamed the hunting grounds, the signs became bad for hunting also. Ey, he had more arrowheads than any three warriors together. Soon everyone called him squaw man."

"He deserved it." At least I was not that weak.

My father shook his head. "Even in this weakest of men there was strength. When the Mexicanos captured his wife and child and took them to be slaves, this man led a war party with his scream for vengeance. Four times his moccasins trod the warpath, and each time he fought with the fury of seven men."

"And then he became a great warrior?" I asked eagerly.

"No, he returned to his arrowheads. Now, in his old age, he is the greatest of arrowmakers."

The old one, Shy Maiden's grandfather! It did not seem possible. But my father had said it, and my father did not lie.

"Now you understand," he said. "In all men, even the weakest, there is strength when the need is great."

Lazy Legs slept. I crept softly into my blanket and thought on my father's words. This was the second time we had talked man to man. I smiled, warmed by the thought of many such talks to come. But I had shared the last campfire with my father.

TWELVE

WE BURN
THE
BLANKET

The night was far gone. From where we camped outside the village we could hear the laughter and chanting of the dances fade and stop. My father had ordered us to wait while he went with the shaman to see Juan José. So we waited, our heads cloudy with sleep, until he returned.

"The chief will listen to nothing now," he said. "We must wait. The feast is tomorrow."

The women smiled. Lazy Legs licked his lips.

"I will not go," I said. "Not with this shame upon my name."

My brother gasped. The women began to chatter, but my father silenced them.

"That is best. Until Juan José has spoken, it is better for you to stay away from the People."

"But the feast," said my mother.

"We will go. I wish to see this trader. One can tell much of a man by the manner in which he gives."

"I will bring you food," whispered my brother. "And if there are knives among the gifts, I will get you one."

"It does not matter," I told him.

But as I sat alone sharpening my knife the next day, I thought of his promise. We had eaten little the night before, and hunger twisted my stomach. When a twig snapped on the trail from the village, I looked up eagerly.

"I am glad you came, brother."

With a laugh the shaman's son stepped into the clearing. I rose slowly, the newly sharpened knife in my hand. He drew his from the top of his moccasin and stepped forward, crouching low.

I told him, "I do not want to fight you now."

"You do not want to fight me ever. Or anyone else." He took another step. "Your blood runs like water at the thought of fighting. You are rabbit-hearted, like your friends the Mexicanos."

"That's not true."

"It is. You treat the enemy like your brother."

That was true. But how did he know of Red Sash and the Papago girl? Then, with his next words, I knew that was not what he meant.

"You eat with him, hunt with him, pretend he is one of the People."

"Lazy Legs is my brother!"

"He's an enemy. When I finish with you, I will kill him. But not as quickly. I will hang him head down over a fire as we do with the enemy. I will laugh at his screams. . . ."

I leaped, knife slashing. He side-stepped. I shot past, stumbled and fell. Grinning, he came at me, the knife ready. I raised myself to one knee and waited. When he lunged, he would be off balance. I dared not move too soon or wait too long. Sweat broke out.

He ran, but it seemed days passed before he reached me. His arm swept down and then up toward my belly. I grabbed the wrist. Weight on one knee, I swung my other leg hard against his. He went down and rolled on his back. Jumping like a frog, I landed with both knees low on his belly. His breath whooshed from his mouth. He lay gasping, his open mouth working.

I raised my knife. Surely now my need was great. Where was the strength my father had said would come? Kneeling over Gian-nah-tah, I knew I could not plunge the knife into that great bear chest. His arms strained my grip. I would not be able to hold him much longer.

Why was he after blood? Because he knew Juan José would decide against him? Because he hated me or wanted to be chief? He twisted under me. I rolled away and sprang to my feet. Again we circled. He lunged. I stepped easily away.

"You could have killed me," he said. "But you are weaker

than a woman. You haven't the strength of a rabbit. You are good for nothing but warming a blanket by the fire."

I dove at him, slashing blindly. He dodged past me and laughed.

"That is more like it. Now we shall have a fight."

Suddenly I understood. Gian-nah-tah had no reason for this fight, except that I was easily angered. Also, I was still weak and the shaman's son was one of those who would always worry and tear at the weak. He was one of those who lived only for fighting. He would not hunt but raid, make war and torture prisoners. In time of peace his presence would make the camp uneasy. He would beat his wife, seek insults where there were none. Anything for a fight, just as he had stung me twice to an angry attack. I straightened and threw my knife on the ground.

"Pick it up," he snarled.

I shook my head. "I will not fight."

"You'll fight!" He came close, swishing the knife at my body, my face and drawing blood on my upper arm. I stared into the trees and did not flinch. If I did not put an end to it now, there would be no stopping Gian-nah-tah's insults until one of us was dead. Killed for no reason except to satisfy his hunger for fighting.

He walked backward, staring at me in bewilderment. He waved the knife and threatened, "This time I will not stop. Pick up your knife."

A small brown figure tumbled from the bushes and ran between us.

"Get away, Little One," I shouted.

She ran to me, holding something in both hands. A gun. One of those worn in the belt. It was new and it was loaded. A shadow fell over it. Gian-nah-tah hissed, staring at the gun in my hand.

"Where did you get this?" He grabbed her shoulders and shook her. "Where did you get it?"

"She can't talk."

"She must. Our people left their guns in their wickiups. The Mexicanos were to leave theirs in the town."

"Perhaps the guns are to be given as gifts."

He laughed bitterly. "The Mexicanos give us guns?"

I knelt beside my sister. "Listen to me, Little One. Were there guns with the gifts?"

She nodded and held up one finger.

"One gun with the gifts?" Another nod. "This gun?"

She shook her head. I looked at Gian-nah-tah, but he did not understand either. I tried again.

"There was only one gun with the gifts?"

She nodded and stretched her arms wide. Her mouth worked and her first words squeezed out. "Big, big gun."

I still did not understand. But Gian-nah-tah knelt beside me and traced a picture in the ground with his knife.

"Is this the gun?" When she nodded, he hissed again. "A soldier's gun. The kind they pull with mules."

I pointed to the gun in my hand. "Are there more of these?"

She nodded and walked about pointing to one spot and then another. Under the blankets, the saddles, the bushes. Guns must be everywhere at the feast. Gian-nah-tah and I stood and stared at each other.

"They have hidden guns," I said. "It is a trap."

"Now it will be our trap." He grabbed the gun from my hand and looked to see if it was loaded.

I pulled my father's gun and ammunition from his blanket and ran after Gian-nah-tah. The big gun thundered. Screams filled the air. Then gunfire. A lot of gunfire—and our People had no guns.

We threw ourselves behind the rise of ground near the Mexicano town and looked down at the feast. Men, women and children littered the ground like limp bundles of old clothes. Near us, in the closed-in place with horses, stood the white-eye Johnson, smiling as he watched the Mexicanos shoot down the crawling wounded.

Gian-nah-tah gripped my arm. "Our chief!"

Juan José ran among the horses. We heard his high cracked voice plead with Johnson to stop the slaughter. With our own ears we heard him call the white-eye friend. And as he said it, the trader Johnson took a gun from his belt and shot our chief through the head. I raised the rifle, but horses moved between it and the trader. I swung round and shot a Mexicano who was raising a hatchet over a woman's head. I had seven shots. Gian-nah-tah had five. When they were gone, I beat my fists against the ground.

"Like shooting rabbits," said Gian-nah-tah. "Just as if they were shooting rabbits."

With his words I remembered the night Lazy Legs and I had slaughtered the rabbits in their sacred dance. I laid my head on my arms and cried. The Little One crept up to me, whimpering. I held her close, not seeing her for my tears. Then I touched Gian-nah-tah's arm.

"Some must have escaped. We must find them."

He nodded and pointed to the mountain behind us. "Up on that cliff is a cave once used by the Ancient Ones. Send all you find up there."

I began to crawl away, but his hand seized my foot. I looked back and saw that he also had wept.

"Take care," he said softly. "We can do nothing to help the ones down there. It is better for us to live and take vengeance. Two warriors can kill a great many enemies."

Tugging Little One after me, I moved off to search the rocks and woods for those who lived.

Juan José's village had been our largest. Two small camps had joined it for the feast. When I counted those huddled in the cave, I found there were only enough to make one village, and not a large one. Many were wounded, for the big gun had been loaded with small bullets, nails, bits of glass and pieces of metal. I walked among them, seeking those I knew. Of my family, only the Little One was there. I stopped by the shaman's son. He stared straight ahead, even when I laid my hand on his shoulder. I at least had the Little One. Gian-nah-tah was alone.

A stone rattled on the mountainside. The huge form of Mangas Colorado filled the entrance of the cave. In his arms, as one might carry a child, was the body of my father. Gently Mangas placed him on the dry earth of the cave. I knelt beside him. His eyes opened and looked into mine. His lips moved. A gourd of water was pressed to my hand.

I lifted my father's head and helped him drink. He lay back and, after a moment, spoke slowly.

"My gun . . . Do not bury the gun with me. . . . You will need . . ." He raised his hand as if reaching for me. "My son."

"I have already used your gun." Suddenly I realized that I had killed two Mexicanos. When the need had been truly great, my strength had come.

My father smiled. From his torn flesh I pulled all the nails and glass I could find, but there was no medicine man to chant and hold back the evil spirits. When the first rays of the sun lit the top of the cave, my father closed his eyes and went away.

I mourned, and my grief struck spark to the flame of vengeance. A flame that blazed from foot to head, lashing the heart and mind to blind fury when we crept back to the feast and saw what the Mexicanos had done. We could not believe it. Soundlessly we crept about the scene of the massacre. Every body had been scalped, even to the smallest baby.

I found my family together. The women had thrown

themselves across my brother, but they had not saved him. They also had been scalped.

Gian-nah-tah paused beside me. "They scalped even their own." He turned his head and spat.

"He was of the People," I said.

"Not to them. They could see he was their own."

I gazed at the unseeing blue eyes and the face that had laughed so often. It was true. The Mexicanos had known and had scalped him just the same. Together we buried them, along with the bodies of the shaman, his wife, the small still form of Shy Maiden, her father and many others. We stood long over the grave of Shy Maiden. When we turned away, we were no longer enemies.

The Mexicanos kept to their town. The men went heavily armed, and no children or women walked the streets. Ey, they had reason to fear! We made our way far into the mountains, moving like a huge turtle in our shell of grief. When our new camp was made, the women and children and old ones safe, then we would cry for vengeance.

The wickiups were built and food collected, but silence hung heavy over the camp. Families were broken. All gathered to eat at one fire. Then we sat together far into the night, stomachs full and hearts empty. It was on such a night that Broken Nose returned from the town of Tucson. He carried a big paper with him. He unrolled it and held it to the light, but Juan José was gone and no one could read the marks.

"I know what they say," said Broken Nose. "I crouched by the wall where it hung and listened to the Mexicanos and the white-eyes read and laugh."

We stared at the big black marks and, as he told us their meaning, it seemed as if we could read them.

$100 FOR APACHE SCALPS

THE GOVERNMENT OF MEXICO

WILL PAY $100 FOR THE SCALP OF A MALE APACHE

$50 FOR THE SCALP OF A SQUAW

$25 FOR THE SCALP OF A CHILD

"Everyone in Tucson is talking of it," said Broken Nose. "The men say they will soon be rich on Apache scalps. The trader Johnson was paid well for his scalps."

"He took them to Tucson?" asked Mangas.

"No, Apache scalps must be taken south of the magic line."

"Apache!" shouted Gian-nah-tah. "How can they call us enemy? They are the enemy."

Broken Nose raised his hand. "There is more. I came through our camp to lead the old ones here. They have gone away. Their scalps are in Mexico."

Apache scalps. It was then we became Apache. Truly, we were the enemy, for no man was our friend.

Mangas led us. In his great mind he carried a plan. We followed it without question. In the dark of night we rode round the town of the traitors and far into the plain below. There we separated. I went with Mangas. We watched the trails Juan José had protected. Every wagon, every horseman, every Mexicano, every dog that moved along the trails was destroyed. Day after day our war cries rang. Blood darkened the sand. Smoke billowed in the sky and the

buzzards gathered. Still we raided and waited. Nothing had gone into the town. No machinery, no food, no ammunition. Soon the Mexicanos must come out or starve. They crept forth at last, the murderers who feasted on Apache scalps.

I do not lie. Over three hundred Mexicano men and women and children began the journey from the town to their cities below the magic line. One by one we cut them down. From every hill, every rock, every cactus came arrows and bullets. They ran, but we were there to meet them. They fired, but they could not see us. Day by day their number lessened. On your fingers and toes you could count the ones who survived, and those we let through to carry the word. To tell the scalpers how the Apache took revenge.

There was peace in our mountains after that. The price of our scalps was not great enough for a man to risk death by fire. I took a wife, a girl from another village, and we had a daughter. We lived the old way and were happy. But the time of peace was short. White-eyes found the Mexicano town and began to dig the copper. They did not ask us for permission, as the Mexicanos had done. They just came, strong and fearless in their walk and talk.

We held council. Gian-nah-tah spoke for war. But Mangas had a plan he wished to try. The same plan he had spoken of to my father long ago. Mangas went to each of the white-eyes and told them where much gold could be found, for the white-eyes pursue gold as coyotes chase rabbits. It was true, and he would have led them there, for the place was deep in the Navajo country. But the white-eyes suspected a trap. I understand why they would think so. Why did they not attack us? Or arm themselves and wait? Never will I understand why they did the terrible thing. It was without reason.

They seized our chief, bound him to a tree and beat him until life was nearly gone. Mangas was a big man to fill with hatred. For every blow they struck, one hundred white-eyes would die.

When his wounds were healed, Mangas received a message from Cochise, our cousin in the Chiricahuas. The white-eyes had slain his brother. Cochise had declared war on the white-eyes. The blue-coated soldiers were marching to the Chiricahua Mountains.

"We will go," said Mangas. "It does not matter where we

kill white-eyes, just so long as we wipe them from the land."

It was the only time our People joined with others to make war. The soldiers brought up big guns, many times larger than the one at the Johnson massacre. Our people were defeated. From then on, no war party numbered more than thirty. Sometimes six or seven. That is true, no matter what the white-eyes say. But it was in this first battle that my cousin's dream showed true.

Fourteen of us were with Mangas. We had cut one soldier off from the rest. Gian-nah-tah shot his horse from under him, and we circled, closing in. The soldier rolled behind the horse and fired one shot. Mangas slumped in his saddle. I yelled to Gian-nah-tah. Riding beside our chief, we supported him until out of danger. Then we lowered him to the ground.

"He will leave us," said Gian-nah-tah.

"No." Who would lead us? There was no one worthy. No one with my cousin's great heart and mind.

"Nothing can save him," said a warrior. "Look at his face. He has gone away."

I frowned, for it reminded me of something, somewhere. Leaping to my feet, I ordered them to put Mangas on a horse. They thought me crazy until I explained my plan. In the dark of night we rode into the Mexicano town and found their medicine man.

"Take out the bullet," I told him. "If our chief lives, we will leave in peace. If you do not save him, every person in this town will die."

It took a long time. The people of the town gathered in their church and prayed to their God. We sat watching the shaman's nervous hands and prayed to Usen. We rode out the next night, leaving the town as we had found it. The leader of our people had been slain. I had returned him to life. My cousin's dream had been true, and Mangas Colorado lived to kindle a blaze of vengeance that Cochise, Victorio and others kept burning.

Season after season we rode and killed and plundered. No longer could the women gather harvests. No longer was there time for hunting. We fled from canyon to canyon, ever searching for safety, ever raiding, ever killing, ever fleeing. All the time my first son grew to manhood the blanket burned with the hot flames of hatred. When it was finished, it was as my father had said. There was nothing left but ashes. For a proud free people, ashes are bitter food.

THIRTEEN

AMONG
THE ASHES

They brought us here, to a land that was not ours. A land they told us we could never leave. They hung tags around our necks and gave us numbers instead of names. On certain days they called us together and counted us like the cattle they drove in for us to eat.

My wife gave me a second son, and I bowed my head in sorrow. What life could he have in this place, in this time?

There were no storage baskets in my wickiup. There were no berries, no mescal to store. Our blankets were tattered, our bows unused. Ey, our teeth were unused also, and our bellies caved in with hunger.

"Come with us and fight," said Gian-nah-tah. "We go to join Geronimo, south of the magic line."

I shook my head. He called me names, but he could no longer rouse my anger. I was like the arrowmaker my father had told about. The need for strength was gone. It is foolish to fight over dead ashes.

But Gian-nah-tah went. And many others. My sister's husband was a scout for the Army and tracked them to their stronghold. The soldiers found them. Geronimo and his followers were taken to a far place called Florida. I wonder if it is like our own country. I hope so. For Gian-nah-tah's bones lie there. It is a terrible thing to leave one's bones in a strange land. I look around the reservation and it is a strange land also. But the white-eyes say it is ours, and that, at least, is a victory.

Not long ago the missionary sent for me. He is a good man, better than most. He has a son the age of mine. They play often together, and the missionary has taken a great liking to my son. On that day he asked me to send my son away to the white man's school in a place called Carlisle. As I listened, I watched the boys playing. The dark head and the yellow side by side. I thought of Lazy Legs and frowned, for it was not clear to me which of these boys was the stranger.

"He is brighter than most," said the missionary. "He learns quickly. He could become a teacher or doctor and do a great deal for your people."

"My people want nothing done for them. That is the trouble. They are used to doing for themselves."

"But the old ways are dead. They must learn the new ways."

"I will think on your words."

I rode to the edge of the reservation, to a hill on which stood a single pine split by lightning. I sat beneath it, looking out over the land that was no longer ours. For two days I sat there, fasting and waiting for the spirits to speak. They came to me at the end of the second day.

"Killer-of-Death," they whispered over and over.

The sun set, turning the clouds to orange and red. The sky was a fiery blaze, like the burning vengeance that had killed our land and the strength of our people. Again the spirits whispered my name. I thought of the sun, also dying in flames but rising again in the morning. At dawn the sky would color again. Not as bright. Not as strong and fiery. But followed by a long bright day. Could it be so with the People? Again the spirits spoke my name. Was I to raise the People as I had once saved our chief?

I thought of the missionary's words and of my son. I thought back to another time, another boy. One who had worried about his weakness toward the enemy. Enemies my son would never know. Just as he would never know the joy that had taken me to a ridge much like this one to thank Usen for giving me life among the People. Truly, it was a different time in which my son was living. And different ways were needed.

I offered hoddentin to the Four Directions. Then I took a piece of a dead tree to give my son. There is no greater charm than the wood of a lightning-riven tree. He would need strong medicine to protect him in the white man's world.

The old horse plodded toward home. Darkness was all about me, but my heart was light.

Format by Nancy Etheredge
Set in Linotype Granjon
Composed by The Haddon Craftsmen, Inc.
Printed by Murray Printing Company
Bound by The Haddon Craftsmen, Inc.
Harper & Row, Publishers, Incorporated